D'Alembert's Principle

ALSO BY ANDREW CRUMEY

Music, In A Foreign Language

Pfitz

D'Alembert's Principle

A NOVEL IN THREE PANELS

Andrew Crumey

PICADOR USA
NEW YORK

For information on Picador USA Reading Group Guides, as well as ordering, please contact the Trade Marketing department at St. Martin's Press.
Phone: 1-800-221-7945 extension 763
Fax: 212-677-7456
E-mail: trademarketing@stmartins.com

Library of Congress Cataloging-in-Publication Data

Crumey, Andrew.
  D'Alembert's principle : a novel in three panels /
Andrew Crumey.
    p. cm.
  ISBN 0-312-19568-0 (hc)
  ISBN 0-312-20401-9 (pbk)
    1. Alembert, Jean Le Rond d', 1717–1783—Fiction. 2.
Europe—History—18th century—Fiction. 1. Title.
PR6053.R76D35 1998
823'.914—dc21

                                                    98-8725
                                                    CIP

First published in Great Britain by Dedalus Ltd.

First Picador USA Paperback Edition: November 1999

10 9 8 7 6 5 4 3 2 1

To Mary and Peter

INTRODUCTION
by John Clute

What you feel when you finish *D'Alembert's Principle* is that you are continuing the book by shutting it. The book which is lying shut upon the lap is now part of the story of a person whose entire body encompasses the lap, but which is not explained or encompassed by the lap, any more than a clock is explained by 3pm. Which is a time upon which a book could easily rest, as upon a lap, while dusk deepens. At the moment this person is me. But whoever reads this introduction, which surrounds *D'Alembert's Principle*, and which was written after the book was read, will shut me too. And a new story will then continue, or has been continuing, outside the book inside it. But we digress. *D'Alembert's Principle*, which is Andrew Crumey's third novel, though it is not exactly fair to call it a novel, is precisely the kind of text which does not end, in the mind's eye, but continues to spin itself. Like this.

And despite the fact it cannot end but only stop, it does still boast a beautiful slingshot ending in which a series of stories within stories – the "Tales of Rreinnstadt" told by an imaginary character in a city whose reality or unreality depends in part upon another book, Crumey's own *Pfitz (1994)*, which is not mentioned by name here though it is quoted from – turns out itself to be told within a book of stories by a man named Müller and entitled *Tales from Rreinnstadt*, which means that the teller of the tales in *D'Alembert's Principle* is actually a character told by the teller of the book of tales within *D'Alembert's Principle*. Then, in the last sentence of the book, the author speaks for the first time in the first person, vouching for nothing, and we stop.

It might be an idea to begin again, with Jean le Rond D'Alembert (1717-1783), whose Principle is as real as he is. As published in his *Traité de dynamique "Treatise on Dynamics" (1743)*, it expands upon Isaac Newton's laws of motion to claim that actions and reactions in a closed system of moving bodies are in equilibrium, a Principle that can be applied in turn to problems in mechanics. In other words, Newton's third law of motion applies to bodies able or "free" to move as well as to stationary objects. According to Crumey's version of the man D'Alembert, whose imagined draft memoirs comprise parts of Book One of *D'Alembert's Principle* "I saw a series of mathematical formulae by which all of the contradictory affairs of men – their whims and passions, and all the pain that this entails – could be reduced to a single principle. . . . So that I could then find some explanation for that question which has caused me [so much] thought and fruitless deliberation . . . ; namely whether the actions of certain people towards me have been out of malice or out of love."

Broad is the descent to Avernus.

Though the consequences of applying the Principle to thought and Story and humans are the central subject matter of the book, *D'Alembert's Principle* is constructed according to another of D'Alembert's concepts, the "*Système Figuré des Connaissances Humaines*", or (roughly) the "Systematic Chart of Human Knowledge and Understanding", which was intended to explain the underlying principles governing the construction of the famous Encyclopedia he edited (1751-59) with Denis Diderot. The Chart is broken down into three main categories: Memory, Reason and Imagination. Under Memory, D'Alembert includes everything that is already known: history; mechanics; technology; etc. Under Reason he incorporates abstract thought of all sorts. And under Imagination he compresses, very offhandedly, all the arts. The three parts of *D'Alembert's Principle* are entitled "Memory: D'Alembert's Principle"; "Reason: The Cosmography of Magnus Ferguson"; and "Imagination: Tales from Rreinnstadt". (As we already know, that third part turns out, as well, though only in part, to be a book called *Tales from Rreinnstadt*.) And except for one circumstance, the whole book could be construed as an hilarious assault upon D'Alembert, his scheme of understanding, and his

Principle by virtue of which human motives can be measured.

Certainly there is an assault. Much of *D'Alembert's Principle* glares upon the interstices of things with the kind of cold eye Luis Bunuel had in his last years as a film director, the years of *The Phantom of Liberty* (1974), which (like this novel) is all about the nature of Story. But it is clear that Crumey also rather loves Jean D'Alembert, whose life story is told in the first part of the novel. D'Alembert is frail, ugly, hysterically witty, and desperately in love with Julie de L'Espinasse (also of course an historical figure). His palpable anguish, his naivety, and his vulnerability, all vividly live on the page. The contrast between the calculus of human behaviour and emotion his Principle claims to provide, and his seemingly total incapacity to perceive L'Espinasse's own passion for another, do not make for laughter. Not exactly. Crumey's portrait of D'Alembert, by far the most sustained character portrait in the novel, is astonishingly tender; but the man is a loon out of Molière; and his Chart is an offense against the human condition; and Crumey's novel constitutes a profound jape against the presumption of the thing.

The second part of *D'Alembert's Principle*, which contains within it a philosophical treatise in the time-honoured form of a Fantastic Journey to the planets, drives the Chart down a steep hill with the brakes off; and the third part crashes the Chart into the realms of Story. Rreinnstadt is the imaginary city constructed in *Pfitz*, and several of the stories told by Pfitz – the Sancho Panza-like servant who was invented by a protagonist of the previous book to occupy an ambivalent role in the invented city – mercilessly and hilariously guy D'Alembert's Principle, which (one must remember) is a device for measuring human nature created by a man for whom Imagination occupies a derisory fraction of the Chart of Human Knowing. The most enthralling of these japes comprises the long description of a clock in the centre of the city, a clock whose innumerable intersecting discs and codes and faces tell so comprehensive a tale of the world that – when a new planet is discovered – its motions are already part of the works. It is, in other words, D'Alembert's version of the principle of Newton's universe made manifest; unfortunately, the citizens of the city spend huge amounts of time attempting to plumb the depths of the clock, uselessly, for the closer they get to any of its workings the more infinitely recursive seems any derivable meaning. In the end it is a clock out of Kafka, or Borges.

At the same time, some of the "Tales From Rreinnstadt" are pure narrative Story, and almost always deal with severed romances, obsessive behaviours which waste entire lives. By echoing D'Alembert's own tragic story, these tales bring us back to the start of things, for the underlying counter-principle within the book which is *D'Alembert's Principle* is *Pfitz*, who may well be "a ghost, or a spirit which had been invoked by malicious and unconstrained story telling". The ghost in the machine is the Story that tells the joke, the Story which returns us to D'Alembert himself, dying of sorrow, dying of a Story he did not have the Imagination to tell. Throughout this astonishing novel, we remember him.

D'Alembert's Principle

I

A woman, her face covered against cold and shame, hurries through the dark streets of Paris on a November night in 1717. She reaches the church of St. Jean le Rond, halts at the steps and carefully places upon them the bundle which she has carried in her arms, and which is myself, her own newborn child wrapped in a blanket.

Only a day earlier, I was nothing more than a small coagulation of unwanted flesh in her reluctant womb; and that flesh was in turn no more than the residue of certain meals, and of a certain act some months previously which might have afforded a brief moment of pleasure to one or other of its participants. I had been brought forth out of inanimate matter, and now I had a soul which my mother wished to destroy. This was the first impulse by which my life was directed. I was like an object repelled by some malevolent force.

I saw it all again, in my dream. False recollections perhaps, reconstructed from the story I learned much later from my foster mother. I don't know how long it may have lasted, nor can I be sure, even so soon after waking, that my memory of what the dream contained is at all accurate, but I believe that while I slept I saw before me not only my birth, but the story of my entire life. I saw a copy of my *Treatise on Dynamics*, that great work of my early years which first brought me fame as a mathematician, and in it the equations had been rewritten in a most wonderful fashion. My life was presented to me as a sequence of propositions, driven by geometrical necessity. I saw a series of mathematical formulae by which all of the contradictory affairs of men — their whims and passions, and all the pain that this entails — could be reduced to a single principle, explained in a few lines of algebra, and hence solved. So that I could then find some explanation for that question which has caused me more thought and fruitless deliberation than any problem of planetary motion;

namely whether the actions of certain people towards me have been out of malice or out of kindness. Whether, for instance, my mother might really have abandoned me in order to prevent some greater evil. And whether the rebuffs which I received some four decades later, from the only woman I ever loved, were motivated by a similar devotion, or else by the most callous selfishness.

My mother wanted only to kill me – I am sure of this. Yes, she wrapped me in a blanket, but it was hardly an adequate form of protection against the cold of the night. It was only providence (by which I mean chance) that caused my rescuer to finish her prayers and make her way out of the church. She told them later that she had a "strange feeling", as if some urgent business needed to be attended to. It was, she maintained, a message from above. Alternatively, she may have heard a noise outside, where I was being abandoned, which prompted her to get up from her knees.

A great empty darkness above me, and then something falling out of that void – a snowflake, perhaps? Something happening, out of that emptiness above me; a blur which my day-old eyes could not resolve. Something growing huge, drawing near. In my dream, the face of an old woman, brought down close to my own. The warmth of her face, close to my own.

It was dark when she stepped outside the church, but still she noticed the little bundle of rags lying on the steps. And she would have thought little of it, except that the bundle seemed to move slightly, as if alive. Then from out of the tangle, a tiny hand, grasping helplessly into the air, and from her lips a gasp of surprise.

"By the blessed Virgin – a child!"

Her fat warm body stooping over the miracle. In my dream, something lowering itself out of the darkness – a finger perhaps. The end of a finger, coming into focus near my face. In my dream, the sweet taste of that finger.

"A baby!"

She picked me up from the steps, held me in her arms in the way that nature had told her a child should be carried, even though she had (I believe) none of her own. A little miracle, she called it. And there would be many theories, about how it was that I had come to be lying there outside the church, but she would maintain that I had been dropped straight from heaven, since I had the peaceful, thoughtful look of an angel. So she picked me up, and I was taken to the Foundling Hospital. And this was how my life began.

II

Downstairs, while their master worked, a conversation was in progress between Henri and Justine, the young married couple who served as D'Alembert's domestic staff.

"He's writing again," Justine said. "Nice to see him doing something useful for a change."

"I'm not so sure, Justine. I don't think it's a good sign."

Henri was older, stouter and wiser. Though hardly past his thirtieth birthday he thought and behaved (particularly with his wife) more like a man of sixty. He had been suspicious of all his masters as a matter of good professional conduct, but for D'Alembert he had always harboured particularly deep reservations. Before his present appointment he had served the Comte de Loges; a man whose excesses were predictable and easily managed. This D'Alembert, however, was a queer old fellow. An intellectual, a bachelor, a recluse. A short, delicate, almost effeminate man, who would write strange symbols on scraps of paper, leave them lying around saying they were something to do with the positions of the planets, so that at first Henri thought he and his young wife must be dealing with an astrologer or necromancer, and he told Justine they should run away before they were both turned into chickens. But D'Alembert was a scientist, not a magician, and a few months after moving in he gave up writing altogether, preferring to spend the days staring dreamily into space. His needs were simple, this should have made him an ideal master, yet still Henri resented him, suspecting him of dark and secret vices (which Henri refused to explain to his wife). She, on the other hand, felt rather fond of the old man. She knew he had been unhappy in love.

Henri was polishing a pair of boots, Justine was boiling eggs for Monsieur d'Alembert's breakfast.

"I hope he isn't going back to all that astrology he was doing."

"It's words he's writing, husband. And what harm can it do if he's keeping himself occupied instead of gazing at the wall all day? Six years we've been with him now, and for the last five of them he's done nothing but mope and shuffle around like a wounded dog."

During those six years the two of them had come no closer to understanding their master than they had been on that first day in 1776 when D'Alembert took the suite to which his academic position entitled him, and Henri and his new wife were appointed to look after him. For Henri it was a promotion, and seeing the state of the old man who was to be his boss he was gratified by the thought that he probably wouldn't last long. D'Alembert had no obvious interests, no distractions, no friends. It was as if he wanted to remove himself from the world completely. Every mirror had been hidden from view, so that he would not have to look at his own face; he wore faded clothes which he would not allow to be replaced, saying he would die in them. During the first year, most visitors were turned away, and so they stopped coming. Even his correspondence dried up like a famished stream. Now it seemed that whatever acquaintances he had, had either forgotten him or were dead.

Justine was ready to take the eggs to the master. "I'd like to know what he's writing," she said brightly.

"I'd say leave him well alone. Perhaps it's a final confession. They do say he's an unbeliever."

Justine scowled. "That's a shocking thing to say! Your own master, too."

"Well I'm your master, Justine, and I'll say what I like. I've never trusted Monsieur d'Alembert, and the less we have to do with him the better."

Justine sighed, picked up the tray and left to go upstairs. Henri finished polishing the boots, which would be left for the master as usual but would probably go unworn. The domestic duties were no more than rituals, carried out more for the sake of those who did them than for their supposed beneficiary. Henri had often felt that he and his wife could pack up and leave without D'Alembert noticing any difference. He had no interest in whether a floor was dusted, whether his food was well prepared, whether or not his bed was warmed. Sometimes Henri even felt a curious nostalgia for the Comte and his raging temper, his violent outbursts if the smallest detail were overlooked. With the Comte everything was straightforward: servants were all out to cheat their masters, they had to be bullied and kept in check. It was hell at the time, but at least you knew what was what. Henri hated and respected the Comte in equal measure, since both these sentiments amounted to the same thing where the nobility were concerned.

And Henri respected Justine too, but in the manner that a father respects the child whom he must educate in the ways of the world. Justine was fifteen when they married, he twenty four. On their wedding night she seemed totally ignorant though not unwilling (he had sometimes wondered over the years if that ignorance was merely feigned in order to reassure him). That they still had no children was a relief in some ways. Justine was both wife and daughter to him, this was the way God willed it and who was he to complain?

He often allowed himself moments for reflection and philosophising during his work. There was so little to do, so much time to think. He knew that the master had written great books and was the cleverest man on earth, but really he was no different from Henri himself, no better. Why shouldn't thoughts pass through a servant's mind which were just as profound as those which occurred to the miserable old fellow upstairs? Were their brains really so dissimilar?

Henri had read one or two books, he'd learned a few things. He knew who Cicero was, and could list the seven wonders of the world. He knew that the earth went round the sun, and the moon went round the earth. Once during an idle moment he imagined D'Alembert as the sun, himself as the earth and Justine as the moon, and he saw in this image an illustration of the cosmic balance of their relationship. So struck was he by this insight that he considered writing it down, even going to find a pen and paper in order to make a start. But when he gazed at the blank sheet the image quickly evaporated, he found that no words could express it. One day, he promised himself, he would note down all his observations, if only he could find the time.

Justine had reached the master's door. She pushed it quietly open and saw his back bent over the desk, his head lowered, no wig hiding his long grey hair. She placed his food on the table near the desk but he did not move, look round or acknowledge her presence. Only the slight trembling of his arm showed that he was neither dead nor asleep, but was writing rapidly.

III

I cannot say for certain where the dream began or ended – indeed, I cannot say for certain whether any dream ever has a beginning or end; we only suppose this to be the case, because we perceive the beginning and end of sleep in other people whom we observe. But I have never been able to identify, in myself, the moment at which sleep (and hence dreaming) begins; nor can I be sure that my first impressions on waking are the true conclusion (and not simply the beginning of awareness after some period of hiatus, or half-sleep). It is not unreasonable to suppose that our dreams may exist within us (or elsewhere) in some complete form, rather like a book, and the act of dreaming consists in leafing through the pages – forwards or backwards – in a way which has no reason or logic to it.

But I do clearly remember my Treatise, rewritten most marvellously. And the idea that in life, as in physics, everything is somehow reducible to a single Principle, a single law or axiom which is self-evident and unquestionable. That human life is not some chaotic event without meaning, but is explicable, and follows hidden rules by which we might make sense of it. It was a dream in which my Treatise was rewritten as my life, or alternatively it was a dream in which the story of my life was presented to me as a kind of mathematical argument. All in the brief time it takes for the head to nod!

I saw many people while I slept, since the picture which my mind presented to me spanned an entire lifetime. But to begin with (if we are to insist on there being a beginning), there was the woman who might be regarded as the prime mover of everything which was to follow. My knowledge of her is entirely second hand (how ironic that such an important figure in my life should be a complete stranger to me); but everything which I have learned about her has led me to admire her talents as much as I despise her character.

Claudine de Tencin was, in her own way, a quite remarkable woman. She tried to quell her passionate instincts early on, and took vows as a nun – but she soon broke them, and embarked on a series of affairs with men who were in one way or another useful to her. These affairs were scandalous even by the jaded standards of our scandalous age, and included (it has been alleged) a liaison with her own brother, whom she promoted through her scheming to the rank of cardinal. There were countless others; the meaningless couplings of a pretty, clever and deeply malicious woman, grown prematurely old with debauchery, whose heart remained untouched by every soul it contaminated. There was even one whom she drove so mad with love for her that he shot his brains out before her eyes, having made known the most bitter accusations against her. That man (Fresnais, I believe he was called) died in vain. Madame de Tencin's career could not be deflected by such a "tasteless" and insignificant gesture.

She found time to write – a pastime which allowed her to demonstrate to the full her intimate knowledge of human weakness. And she held one of the most prestigious salons in

Paris. Marmontel, Fontenelle . . . they all kissed her hand, in those days of splendour.

Whether Madame de Tencin regarded her affairs as a sideline of the salon, or whether it was the other way round, I cannot say. Most important however, from the point of view of my own story, was her liaison with the chevalier Destouches, a man who was very handsome, very dull, but nevertheless had a touch of decency quite unusual in Parisian society. They each of them made their appearance, in my strange dream (that strange Treatise); she as a great, malevolent ellipse, whilst he was a tangent to some other kind of conic section (a hyperbola, I believe). And I saw them (during those minutes or hours when I dozed) coming together in their brief moment of intersection.

How the affair began, I cannot say. Madame de Tencin's hectic course through the noblemen of this country and several others had no particular logic to it; it was, I suppose, nothing more than chance which should have united them. And I can only guess at the circumstances under which I was conceived by them.

For so it was. Those two people reluctantly caused me to be brought forth into the world – she was the one (though I only found out many years later) who carried me through the cold streets of Paris one November night in 1717 and abandoned me on the steps of St. Jean le Rond, calmly leaving me to almost certain death.

And it was chance also, which having given me unwanted birth now also chose to save me, by bringing that old woman who happened to come out of the church (a fat woman, with a warm face; this much I am sure I can somehow remember). And so I was rescued, and carried to the Foundling Hospital.

How did that Hospital appear in my dream? As a great grey hull of screaming infants, a dismal place lined from wall to wall with the countless little O's of wailing mouths, like the notation of some astronomical number huge beyond reckoning. It is fortunate that I did not have to spend very long there.

Madame de Tencin heard that I had been saved, and thought no more of the matter (even when I became celebrated, she still would never acknowledge me or show any interest in my existence). The dull chevalier, on the other hand, was quite shocked when word reached him of the child of his which now lay side by side with all the other abandoned waifs of Paris. He arranged at once that I should be removed from there and sent to foster parents. It was an act of decency and of unwitting kindness, since he sent me to two of the dearest people one could imagine.

Monsieur Rousseau was a glazier; his wife had recently lost her own child, and took me to her breast with a force of goodness equal and opposite to the repulsion of my natural mother. In that wonderful translation of my Treatise, her unconditional love and kindness appeared as a sort of axiom; a thing which could not be proved, but was stated as being beyond question. And it was my foster parents who coined for me the name I have always borne and which commemorates the place where I was found: Jean le Rond d'Alembert.

I have often had cause to wonder how, if I had not been abandoned but had instead been brought up by the cynical and malevolent Madame de Tencin, the course of my life might then have gone. Would I still have risen to become the most famous mathematician in France, honoured by every scientific society in Europe? Would I have found myself labouring with Diderot on that great effort, the *Encyclopédie*, with which I wasted some of the best years of my life? And would I have fallen, with the same tragic naivety, into that pitiful state of devotion for a woman fifteen years my junior – a woman who would spend the last years of her life deceiving me, and betraying all the love which I bestowed upon her?

In my dream, as I recall it further, I see once again that first manifestation of natural geometry, as it appeared to me all those years ago. I see myself as a young child (no more than three years old) sitting on the floor, while the sunlight falls

crumpled from the flawed pane in the window above me. I
watch the pattern which the light makes upon the floor;
ripples of brightness, where the sunshine has been distorted
in its flight. By some mysterious process, the falling light is
creating an image, or at least an interpretation, of the imperfect pane through which it has passed.

It must have been then that my passion for understanding
the ways of nature first took root. What was it made of, this
light which fascinated me? And how could it be bent and
folded like this, by a wrinkled pane of glass? Another
memory: standing beside the great oak dinner table which
seemed huge, dark and mighty by comparison with my small
body. Upon the table – at the level of my eyes – a drinking
glass stood in the bright light of the sun. I remember
watching the sparkling motes of dust floating around it; bil-
lowing when I breathed gently upon them. And the glass
itself, brilliant in the sunlight. The light was focussed by it
somehow: on the table, the glass had cast a wonderful pattern
– a bright cusp of captured sunlight. How were such things
possible?

Those early years were as vivid in my dream as they are in
my waking recollection. The whole world huge and unex-
plored around me, like a text waiting to be read and understood. My eagerness to grow and learn, even in my games.
And accompanying all of this, the memory of my foster
mother. Watching her pour water, steaming hot, into a metal
bath, the steam rising and curling. All of this was a warm and
subtle mystery: the bath, its texture, curvature, the sheen of its
surface. The plumes of steam, curling and folding (why
should steam do this?). My foster mother's great breast beneath the crisp whiteness of her blouse, her smile as she
turned and looked down from the lofty height of her love
and wisdom at my own small face. Beneath all of this, some
great answer lay waiting to be perceived.

When I was four I was sent to boarding school, an experience which almost succeeded in quelling my curiosity forever. My natural father, the dull chevalier, had provided

money for my upbringing and education, and the school I was sent to was of a kind considered respectable. Indeed, I am sure that an education such as I received there would be ideal for anyone who intended to make their future career in politics or the church, or some other area requiring the blind acceptance of orthodoxy, and a total lack of originality of any kind.

From the start I loved mathematics. Even as I learned to count, I could see that here was the true language of nature – not the A,B,C of the reading master. Words were no more than tokens of exchange; numbers on the other hand had a value that was eternal and unalterable. As I grew older, my skill increased in the games I could play with these wonderful toys I had discovered. Mathematics provided an avenue of escape for my frustrated imagination, and in my spare time I would explore those problems which were declared to be too advanced for our study. In this way, I soon came to find my classroom lessons trivial by comparison with my private investigations.

I resented the arbitrary discipline and pointless ritual of the place, but I accepted them quietly – for it has always been my way to avoid confrontation if at all possible, and resist in ways that are less direct. I must, in fact, have seemed like a model pupil, since I was bright and did well, though really I longed for nothing more than to grow up, to be accepted as a human being, and to be out of the place.

I was a small child – just as I would later grow into a small man, physically weakened by the trauma of my birth and abandonment, and I learned early on how best to deal with such a disadvantage in life. There was no point trying to fight back whenever I was teased; the result would only have been a thorough beating by boys far stronger than me. And so I deflected the threats of others through my wits.

There was one whom we all feared more than any other. He was known as the Bear because of his size and mean temper. From my first days at the school I knew of him, as did everyone; a boy who inspired terror wherever he went. He achieved this in the manner of all bullies; by threat more than by actual violence. If he did rough up a boy who crossed his path, it was always with the help of his lackeys.

The Bear must I suppose have taught me a great deal about the workings of the human world. I probably learned more from watching him than from the lessons of the school-masters, perhaps more even than from all the great books I have read. The Bear was a big fellow, and slow witted, and these two factors had done much to shape his character. He could not win friends through kindness, and so he had instead learned to make everyone fear him. How many Kings, Generals and even nations are driven by similar impulses, the product of the accidents of birth?

The Bear was usually escorted by two boys, each of them much smaller and much brighter than their master. In this way they formed a kind of team, each compensating for the others' defects. They were not evil boys, but they were weak and insecure, and this led them to do many evil things.

I once saw them teasing a child three or four years younger than themselves, and half their size. I must have been about ten at the time; I was making my way across the court-yard, and as I rounded the corner I saw them torturing their victim behind the chapel wall, where they would not be discovered by the masters. The three were surrounding the child, the Bear was making little stabbing movements towards him, without actually hitting him. I could hear the voices of the other two. "Haven't they told you, Pierre? Your mother is dead."

"No! It's a lie!"

"What? You call us liars?"

The Bear pulled the little boy's bonnet from his head and threw it onto the sand. I could hear the child sobbing. As he stooped, weeping, to pick up the hat, the Bear kicked him to the ground. He was a small child, but he landed heavily with a thump and a cloud of dust. It must have been fear or surprise which checked his tears now. The three of them began to kick him as he lay on the ground.

"We're no liars! Say you're sorry."

If the child made any reply, it would not have been heard. The Bear had pushed his two companions aside so as to enjoy the glory of this moment.

"Kill him!" they were saying, "Finish him off!"

On the face of the Bear, I could see a kind of ecstasy; a look of grim pleasure, like the face of an animal as it prepares to feast on its prey. The Bear could hear nothing, see nothing; it was no longer a boy whom he was kicking, but a bundle of rags no better than the one my own mother had chosen to deposit on some cold steps. In the face of the Bear I could see no evil, no hatred. This was what filled me with such terror. For the Bear, love and hate, joy and sorrow, were two sides of a valueless coin which he could spin and let fall without caring which face might land uppermost.

"Say you're sorry!" Still the lackeys were barking, and I watched from far off, too terrified to intervene but just as much a part of the crime. If they looked in my direction, they would probably do the same to me.

At last the Bear grew bored. He straightened his clothes with absurd dignity, and he and his companions left the scene. It had all lasted no more than a minute or two.

The boy lay in the dust, sobbing again gently, his nose and forehead bleeding. As I went over to him, what words of comfort could I offer? I have, during the subsequent years, read many stories of school bullies and their victims. In the stories, the victim secretly learns to fight, training patiently and waiting for revenge. Then when he is ready he challenges the bully to a duel, wins an easy victory, and the power of the bully at once evaporates. I have read this story many times, but I have never seen it occur in life. Rather, the story I have witnessed again and again is the one I saw then of victimisation, and the stoical acceptance of suffering. The child who had been beaten was smaller than his attackers, and though I was older than him I was hardly taller. Had either of us tried to resist, the Bear and his friends would have thrashed us with even greater relish. I helped the child to his feet.

"I want my mummy," he said.

I helped him tidy himself up, though later he was chastised by the masters for his appearance, and gave the excuse that he had tripped up while watching geese fly overhead. This flickering of a child's imagination, even in the midst of suffering, has remained vividly in my memory over the years. He was a frail, sensitive child, and I believe he died of cholera before his fifteenth birthday.

The only way to survive the wrath of the Bear was to avoid any confrontation with him. Like all the others, I tried never to go anywhere alone if it might take me onto his territory. To relieve the sense of fear I felt, I would entertain the other boys with my imitations of the Bear, his slow drawling voice and heavy movements. Their applause and uneasy laughter reassured me, and made me feel that I had won their respect, even if I was small and weak.

We were a dormitory of twenty boys, easily enough to overpower the Bear, to bring him to his knees and give him a beating he would never forget. Yet we never dared. Whole nations have behaved thus, awed by the power of tyrants.

There was to be no salvation for us, no happy resolution to the story. The Bear continued his reign of terror, eventually growing up and joining the civil service where he had a distinguished career. Years later I happened to see him at a dinner, a high ranking official now. He showed no sign of remembering me. Even then I thought of revenge, as I watched him eating his soup.

IV

"I do believe I heard him laughing," Justine said when she met her husband again downstairs. "There must be something in his writing which he finds amusing."

Henri shrugged. "Laughter is a sure sign of madness. Anyone with any sanity knows that there's little to smile about in this life."

"Oh Henri, you old pessimist."

"That's a big word for you, my dear. Have you been reading books again?"

"What if I have?"

Henri felt the shiver of a distant threat. Justine had a look of playful defiance in her eyes.

"Just remember your place," he told her.

"As if I could ever forget it! But don't forget, husband, that it's me that keeps you in your place just as much as you keep me in mine."

"What on earth do you mean by that?"

"What I mean is that while the roof may hold the pillar from swaying, it's the pillar that stops the roof from falling down."

Henri was scratching his head, his jaw hanging open. "What the devil are you talking about, woman? What have pillars and roofs got to do with anything?"

Justine smiled, and put her arm around her husband's neck. "What I mean is that the earth needs the moon and the moon needs the earth." He had told her once of his striking cosmic idea, and was surprised that she had remembered and even apparently understood it, in her own simple way. He nodded, reassured by the thought that he had taught her so well.

"Sometimes I almost think you should have been born a man," he said. It was the highest compliment he could pay her.

"I often wish I was," she replied.

Henri had several errands to attend to, which would keep him out for much of the day. Meanwhile Justine would carry on with her usual domestic routine. She took the bucket and brushes upstairs, ready to begin sweeping and cleaning.

The apartment was made all the grander by its emptiness, the lack of any visitors who might make it seem something other than a mausoleum. This emptiness, though, was what she liked most. Going about her daily duties without interruption, she could find time for herself and her own thoughts. The library was her favourite place. It had been Monsieur d'Alembert's exclusive preserve during the first months after he took up residence, but then he had ordered that a large number of books be taken to the study where he might be able to consult them more easily, and since then he had hardly bothered to visit the grand room with its vast store of neglected volumes. He had drawn up a list of those books which were to be relocated, and it was Henri who had found them all on their shelves, not wishing to entrust such an important and highly technical task to his wife. Justine, on the other hand, had been given the job of actually moving the cases of books, which were very heavy and had to be dragged along the polished floors.

At that time, five years ago, she had never seen so many books, or dreamed that they could weigh so much. Stopping to catch her breath, she had pulled one of the volumes from the case where it lay, opening its pages at random. She had seen tiny print in an unknown language, and engraved pictures whose meaning she could not fathom. Something like a sea-shell, or a kind of vegetable perhaps. Then she saw at the rim of the unknown object the recognisable lines of a human ear. The illustration showed the inner workings of the organ, a mysterious coil or tube, and structures like the mechanical parts of a clock. She turned to other pages, saw an eye sliced through, the inverted image of a flame projected onto its rearmost wall. Then as she continued leafing through the book she had to stifle a gasp of surprise, for what she found was a picture of a naked man, every detail rendered with a precision which stunned her so utterly that she felt no urge to laugh, but was filled instead with a sense of profound and unnerving awe. Looking at the naked figure, she had tried to compare it with what little she had seen of Henri whenever he undressed fully, the only light remaining being that of the moon and stars, though sometimes even these would be shuttered out by her modest husband. Her own mental picture of his body was a tactile one. She knew that he could be flaccid or else large and rigid, but she could gauge this change only by touch (never the touch of her hands, which she had attempted once but been thoroughly scolded for it). Touch, and the strength of her own imagination. She knew Henri's private regions in the way that she knew the shape of her back teeth, over which she would run her tongue, or knew the ridge of her own tired back beneath her hand.

The picture she had seen was a confirmation, yet also a disappointment. The neatly engraved stub of flesh looked no more wonderful or mysterious than a finger, while it was the dissected ear and eye which remained fixed in her mind as inner continents of unimagined complexity and beauty. Seeing the naked man made whole was simply a case of recognising what had previously been guessed at, and finding it to be hardly worthy of so much speculation. It was through precisely such speculation, however, that she would often remind herself that she belonged to no-one, that her thoughts were free no matter how oppressive her life might sometimes feel.

She had sat on the floor of D'Alembert's library and flicked through the rest of the anatomy book, the text incomprehensible but the illustrations merely increasing her thirst for knowledge rather than quenching it. She saw a foetus snugly curled in the womb of its mother, the picture made her recoil and wonder if a real woman had been cut open to enable such a drawing to be made, or whether the drawing was an illustration of how the child should be removed under certain circumstances. She had heard of such cases, and the thought of them made the prospect of pregnancy all the more dreadful. At that time it was only eighteen months since her marriage, but five years later she would still feel relieved to have escaped (so far) the risks of pregnancy; a stroke of luck for which she had come to be sure that Henri was responsible. She now wished she could consult once more the book which resided on Monsieur d'Alembert's shelf, to try and find how one might confirm the issue.

There had been other books to look at before she dragged the heavy case to the study; some in foreign languages, or else filled with the symbols of what she already knew to be mathematics, but others with texts which she could understand. She had so little time to try and find out which of all the books in the library D'Alembert regarded as important enough to move close to his desk. What might make them so significant? Among them all there was no Bible, nor anything which might be devotional in nature. Instead there was a great deal of science and nature, illustrations of everything imaginable; a workshop in a knife factory, the robed people of an African tribe. Mountains, rivers, distant kingdoms. There were volumes of drama, of verse, and romances some of whose authors she had heard of. There was an entire universe of thought, even in a single packing case! It felt somehow lighter, when she finally pulled it, since she herself felt light with its wisdom.

Since that first day of discovery, Justine had visited the library as often as she could. D'Alembert never went there now; the only obstacle was lack of time and the fear that Henri might discover her. Over the years she had come to know the system by which the books were shelved. One case held a great many volumes of stories which she read for diversion, while another was devoted to speculations on every conceivable subject. She had even read in one of them that some wise men questioned the existence of God, and the everlasting nature of the soul, and this threw her into an agony of doubt which lasted some weeks, and which she could only explain to her husband as a "woman's problem"; a description which was always sufficient to quell any further enquiry.

Today she was going to continue reading about the conversion of Constantine. She had memorised the page number as usual, rather than risk leaving any mark of her intrusion. She swept the floor of the library very swiftly, then put the broom beside the door and went to fetch the book, looking again towards the door before positioning herself beyond the scope of its view. She crouched on the floor and opened the book on her lap, but soon found that she was in no mood to read.

She was thinking about Monsieur d'Alembert. He had suddenly taken up writing again, he might choose to return to the library where he would find her idling, and then she would be dismissed, she and Henri would be ruined. What might the master be writing, alone in his study?

She thought she heard a sound, she closed the book

swiftly, her heart racing. She stood up and put the book back in its place, but soon realised there was no-one outside. She went to the door, picked up the broom and looked along the corridor. Might the old man be walking around? Perhaps it was only Henri leaving.

Justine continued her cleaning route, looking round all the time to see if anyone might be about, until she reached the study. Pushing the door further open to look in she saw D'Alembert still at his desk, the great desk he had long ago ordered to be turned round so that he need never look towards the door to see the staff enter and leave, but might instead work in peace in the illusion that he was completely alone. His food remained untouched. To think, to study and write; Justine envied D'Alembert, no matter how much sorrow and anger he might feel, and for whatever reason. Earlier she had heard him laugh, as if at his own work, but she knew the laugh was a hollow one. His purpose was serious, he made no sound now. Letters and documents lay scattered beside him on the desk, others were strewn on the floor. When she went in to pick up the tray of food, he showed no sign of noticing her.

V

In 1729, when I was twelve, I was sent to the famous Mazarin College, and here I began to find stimulus from teachers who seemed to understand mathematics better than I did at that time. But still I resented those long hours spent studying such useless topics as ecclesiastical history, or the brutal exploits of tyrants and conquerors, people no different from the Bear, whose only achievement was to have brought misery and suffering wherever they went. Long hours, which I would have preferred to devote to my own calculations. I have never had any interest in history as it is presented in the textbooks – the dull and pointless cataloguing of events considered great simply because of the high rank of their participants. The only history which interests me is the record of those who have achieved something through their own worth and ingenuity.

At the College, one of the masters was a particular favourite of mine. He had, I believe, done some original mathematical work of his own; he was no mere reciter of facts, but had an understanding of what he told us, and this made his lessons far more interesting than most. He was a short, plump man, always breathless, and although in his thirties or forties he had the face of a boy, which was perhaps what was so endearing about him. One day he said, almost as if the thought had only just occurred to him, "Imagine a ship sailing steadily across the sea."

I saw in my mind one of the vessels whose illustrations I had admired in a book of travels (I had never seen the sea at that time).

"Now tell me," said the master, "what is the speed of the ship during a single instant of time?"

Various answers were suggested, but most of us agreed in the end that since a moment of time has no duration the ship would travel no distance, and hence its speed during that single instant was zero.

The master beamed. "But this would then mean that at all moments the ship is stationary! In which case, how can it be moving?"

It was a paradox; one which, the master told us, had first been considered by Zeno of Elea some two thousand years earlier. My teacher offered a solution which left me unconvinced; I resolved to think deeply about the matter. Eventually I was to discover that the problem had already been answered by Newton, and his method of resolving it, the theory known as the calculus, would be the main instrument of all my subsequent research into the behaviour of solid bodies, of fluids, and of the stars and planets. That all types of motion, and hence all of Nature itself, could be reduced to some huge problem of calculus, was an idea which could lead one to suspect that here might be that Great Truth, the single law which must underlie everything we see. Already I realised, in those early years, that in this new vision of the cosmos it might even be the case that there would be no place left for God.

My dream may not have proceeded in a strictly chronological fashion through the events of my life, but I feel certain that in the curiously rewritten Treatise I saw before me, those achievements to which I owe my fame and which occupied the first three decades of my existence appeared as little more than lemmata, anticipating the main results to follow. So now let me summarise them.

After leaving the College I returned to live with my foster mother Madame Rousseau (her husband having since passed away), and spent some time studying law and medicine, as I had been persuaded that I would in this way be led into a dignified career. But mathematics continued to beckon, and I spent every spare hour in the public library. I would only have time to memorise certain results from the great mathematicians of the past – the rest I had to derive and prove for myself. And I began working seriously on problems of calculus applied to planetary motion.

In 1739, at the age of twenty two, I submitted my first paper to the Académie des Sciences. Two years later I was enlisted by them as astronomical correspondent, and my career progressed rapidly. 1743 saw the publication of my *Treatise on Dynamics*, the great work which first brought me fame. In it I presented an important principle by which (using the theory of calculus) all kinds of motion can be reduced to a calculation involving stationary bodies. The following year I generalised my results to cover flowing water and the currents of the air, and so I gave a general account of the elementary laws which govern the phenomena we observe in nature.

I also studied a problem which had been causing confusion since before the days of Newton. What rule might govern the shape of a vibrating string as it oscillates? My debate with Euler on this subject would go on for years, but all would agree on the validity of the differential equation which I first wrote down in 1744.

And so by now the abandoned child has grown into a man; a short, slightly comical man, who delights in amusing others, for he has never forgotten the taunts he received at school. A man with a voice so high as to be regarded by some as falsetto, and bearing a face which is not by any means handsome (and is on occasion maliciously described as somewhat feminine), but who has nevertheless the capacity to mimic those who take themselves too seriously, and who can bring laughter and amusement to any gathering. And already I was rapidly becoming the most celebrated mathematician in France.

A meeting of the Academy took place at which a young man of about my age, recently arrived in Paris, presented a paper outlining a new method of musical notation. The man was named Jean-Jacques Rousseau (no relation, of course, to my foster parents), and he proposed an ingenious system employing numbers instead of the usual stave and notes. Rameau disapproved; nevertheless I saw some merit in the idea.

Rousseau was earning a living as a music teacher, but was eager to become a part of Parisian intellectual life. He had already knocked on many doors, letters of introduction in hand, before I first saw him. After the meeting he seemed dejected by the committee's apparent lack of enthusiasm, but his mood brightened considerably when I offered to write my own introduction on his behalf. When he next contacted me the following year, he had already established himself. He was proposing to found a new periodical, to be named *Le Persifleur*, and asked if I would be willing to contribute. His partner in the venture was to be one Denis Diderot, and I arranged to meet the two of them for dinner.

They could hardly have been more dissimilar; Rousseau the cautious melancholy introvert, Diderot the garrulous polymath whose conversation constantly hopped from one subject to another. They dined regularly together (along with Condillac), and I arranged to meet them at the Palais Royal, from where we would go to eat at the Panier Fleuri nearby. I arrived early, and waited alone. After some minutes Rousseau appeared, apologising far too profusely (for he was also early himself). His excessively guilty conscience was a characteristic I would grow to find a little tiresome. Condillac was ill, apparently; there was only Diderot to wait for.

Almost half an hour passed before he made his appearance. During this time Rousseau explained how his friend was always very bad at keeping appointments, but never missed one of their weekly dinners. From this I concluded that not only must Diderot be erratic and untrustworthy, but that he must also be devoted more to good food than to the well-being of his friends. Though the forceful charm of the man I was about to meet would make me forget this opinion for many years, I would ultimately find that my original assessment was indeed correct.

At last Rousseau's face lit up. "Here he is! Denis!"

A large man strode towards us, who could easily have been a hall porter. He wore no wig, and his fair hair hung down over the collar of an old overcoat which looked as though it needed mending (or, better, throwing out). His breeches were stained and faded, while his stockings were stitched and darned in a manner which made no effort to hide the fact. He looked like a vagabond, and yet he was extraordinarily handsome. I felt at once that here was a man who could not enter a room without every head turning to admire him.

"Jean-Jacques! Early as usual, eh?" He gave Rousseau a great hug which seemed to lift him off his feet. "Have you seen *Perseus* yet, as I told you? Such music! And the sets are magnificent."

Rousseau ignored this (I would come to learn that he never commented on any opera unless he felt sure that it was inferior to the works which he himself wrote). Instead he quietly introduced me to Diderot, who had as yet hardly noticed me. Suddenly Diderot's manner changed. As he turned to acknowledge me he seemed to shrink.

"It is such an honour, sir. I know much of your work; I have read your Treatise and found it . . . a masterpiece." He threw his broad hands into the air as he spoke.

39

Diderot, I had learned from Rousseau, earned a meagre living by teaching, translating and writing articles of one kind or another. Though he was an atheist, he had studied for a Doctorate in theology, then gave it up for law, then gave this up too to lead a life of private study and indiscriminate socialising; his allowance from his father (a worthy cutler in Langres) having been cut off. He found easy work as a private tutor in mathematics; a subject which he himself was trying to master, and in which at first he could only keep one or two lessons ahead of his pupils. If they were bright they really had no need of him, and if they were dull then no amount of coaching would help. Diderot's attitude was therefore that of the gardener who puts all his trust in the mercy of the weather and the forces of natural growth.

He wrote sermons (having sold a number to departing missionaries); he hung around the theatre, even when he couldn't afford to get in, and dreamed of becoming an actor. He was, like Rousseau, a man full of ideas who lacked only fame, and this would come in time.

We went to eat. I had never dined at the place, but it seemed a little too good for my impoverished companions, so that I wondered if I would be expected to foot the entire bill. "Monsieur Diderot," the waiter exclaimed, "how good to see you again!" I concluded that despite his poverty Diderot knew how to tip well. Then I became even more worried when he took us to a private room and ordered a feast which included braised thrushes and asparagus, and fine wine.

Diderot saw the expression on my face as the wine was poured. "Sir, you can tell I am not a wealthy man. But I received payment today for a translation; a big book and a big sum," he laughed, and swallowed half the contents of his glass. "So now we shall eat it all up. Eat! Eat! Eat!"

He had the coarseness of a ringmaster. When the food arrived he picked up pieces of it with his own hands, smearing his lips and often speaking with his mouth full of food. I could tell that he was starving, that he probably hadn't had a proper meal for several days. Nevertheless, the tone of his conversation remained incongruously cultured.

"Monsieur d'Alembert, I would be grateful if you could explain to me a few points which I didn't understand in your Treatise."

When he had complimented me earlier I had taken it to be no more than polite flattery, but Diderot asked a number of questions which showed that he really had read the work quite carefully. He explained to me his passion for mathematics, in which he was completely self-taught.

"Mathematics is what I shall always keep coming back to," he said. "It's my intellectual home."

I realised that despite his manner, Diderot was a kindred spirit. The conversation traversed a great number of subjects with dizzying speed, until suddenly Diderot was telling us a story about his school days.

"The trouble is that I am a big fellow, I always have been. One's physique determines so much in life." I shuddered with silent agreement. He continued, reaching across the table for a sauce dish; "If I gave the merest push to a lad then it inevitably became a punch, such was my size and strength. Do you call an elephant a bully if it happens to trample a few creatures whom it doesn't even see? Well, I'm afraid that at school I became known as something of a ruffian. But I was also very good at my work, and earned a number of prizes. Then when the prize-giving day arrived, I was banned from the school because of my supposed crimes against a fellow who thoroughly deserved everything I gave him." He bellowed loudly, slapping the back of Rousseau, who was pecking quietly at his food like a bird. "Well, I was having none of that. I showed up for the ceremony, but at the gate the porter spotted me and chased after me with a stick. I escaped and got in, but not before he had managed to give me a blow to the hand which drew blood. So at last I went and took all my prizes with an injured hand, shaking blood onto the one who congratulated me. What a scene, eh? But that was nothing compared to what I had to endure before I could marry my little Nanette." Then he turned to me again. "Do you play chess Monsieur d'Alembert?"

The sudden change of topic confused me. I told him I knew the rules.

"Then you must play Jean-Jacques. He beats me every time. I think he only keeps playing me because he's so fond of winning."

Rousseau gave a look of disapproval.

"You see," Diderot went on, "Jean-Jacques regards the entire world as a contest."

I could tell that Rousseau's hackles were rising. "And how do you see the world, Diderot?" he asked pointedly.

Diderot sat back in his chair and mopped the corners of his mouth. "I see the world . . . as a banquet!" He laughed so heartily that he began to choke, and for a moment I thought that he might be about to drop dead before us. Rousseau slapped his back and he recovered.

"Monsieur d'Alembert," Diderot said solemnly, "You are a very distinguished man, even though you're so young. But one day the three of us will be very famous indeed, I swear it! I don't say it because I'm drunk. I am drunk, of course, but even if I were not it would still be true that the three of us together . . ." he stood up, swaying, "the three of us represent the whole of philosophy. Rousseau is music, the theatre; you Monsieur d'Alembert are mathematics and science . . ." Diderot paused, then sat down.

"And what are you?" I asked him.

He finished another glassful of wine and looked at me with unsteady eyes. "I, sir . . . am Diderot. Ha!"

I confess that at the time I found his words vain and somewhat pitiful. He was four years older than me (that is to say, already past thirty), and if he was to make his mark on the world then he knew he had to hurry. He was in fact already working on various philosophical ideas which he hoped to turn into a book. In those days, of course, everyone wrote "philosophy" of one kind or another. Diderot's was one wholly lacking in system or rigour; it was, in fact, a perfect reflection of the man himself. In this respect he was indeed a true *philosophe*. But Diderot was quite right; the three of us were to become very famous indeed.

"I don't intend to spend the rest of my life translating the works of others," he said. "I want to write, and to write well."

"An admirable ambition," I told him. "But what about this periodical of yours? That is, after all, the reason why I'm here."

"Oh, we can speak of that another time. But now let's drink to friendship and philosophy."

By the end of the meal I had watched Diderot drink two and a half bottles of wine while Rousseau and I had shared one. Yet Diderot had not become any more intoxicated. I realised that his exhilaration was caused more by the food in his stomach and the pleasure of conversation. He insisted that we go with him to his house to play chess, but on the way there Rousseau made his excuses and bade us good night.

"You'll still come won't you, Monsieur d'Alembert?" There was a pleading, childlike look in Diderot's eyes. He gripped my hands imploringly. Of course, I said.

While we walked in the cold night air he stopped and turned to me. "I still haven't asked how you see the world, Monsieur d'Alembert."

The question was made seriously, and so I gave him a serious answer. "I see it as a system obeying certain laws which must be discovered through careful analysis."

"Mathematics is so wonderful," I heard Diderot murmur.

We walked for a considerable time. "Is it much further?" I eventually asked. In fact it was; Diderot, after the excesses of our dinner, could not afford a cab. I offered to pay, and we found a driver who took us.

Diderot's home was on the third floor of a dismal building in a poor and disreputable area. Inside I found an ill-lit room over which hung the disagreeable odour of earlier cooking. In a corner sat an elderly woman who turned out to be Diderot's mother in law. She was mending some lace, and said nothing. Then his wife appeared from another room, and seeing me she addressed her husband.

"Is this gentleman one of your friends from the Régence?"

"No, little wife, this man is the greatest mathematician since Newton!"

The room was kept barely warm by a stove in the corner. The most obvious furnishing was a huge bookcase crammed from top to bottom, and a rough table beside it where Diderot could work. These alone distinguished the place from the habitation of a labourer, which it would otherwise have resembled perfectly. I saw a plate of food half eaten, some clothes drying near the stove. The scene was little better than squalid. Why then did I feel such a curious envy for Monsieur Diderot and his humble home? Was it because I saw a simple domesticity which I could never have?

Madame Diderot asked her husband where the rest of the money was, and he looked at me awkwardly.

"Surely you haven't spent it all? Denis, how could you?"

"But look Nanette, I bought you a present." From out of his pocket he brought a crumpled piece of light blue ribbon. She seemed consoled by this.

"We're going to play chess now," Diderot told her. "You don't have to wait up for us." He brought out a board and a set of pieces, and the two women left us without a word. Diderot placed the pieces, keeping his eyes on the board as he spoke. "I take it you're unmarried?" he said. I told him yes. "Then stay that way. Believe me, it's for the best. Don't get me wrong, I love Nanette, I even went to prison for her, oh yes. You don't believe me? Well, it's true. My own father obtained a *lettre de cachet* against me rather than let me marry her. I was put in a monastery," he laughed. "Jumped out the window and ran away to Paris. Father still doesn't know we're man and wife."

We began to play.

"But marriage is a bad thing," he went on. "It's an unnatural institution. It's less than a year and already I'm looking at other women again. I don't make her happy, you can see that."

We continued the game in silence, and our mutual concentration brought about a bond between us much firmer than that which our conversation had achieved. At last Diderot won.

"Wait till I tell Rousseau!" he laughed. "But never mind sir, life is not a contest, is it?"

I agreed. In the course of the evening I had grown fond of Diderot. He was like a great child; he could neither be judged good nor bad, since he seemed to inhabit a world outside all conventional rules. He lived in a universe of his own making, disordered and chaotic, but perfectly suited to his needs.

It was very late. "Stay here!" Diderot said. He explained that they were used to having guests; there was always someone who was being thrown out by their landlord or their spouse, and a spare mattress was permanently at the ready. I told him that my foster mother would wonder what had happened to me. I had never spent a night away from home.

"Never?" He looked at me with incredulity. "Not once?"

I could not be persuaded to stay. He saw me downstairs, insisting that we must meet again, that he hoped I regarded him now as my friend, which I did. We shook hands warmly, and I went out into the night, walking randomly in search of a cab, and deliriously happy.

The proposed periodical never emerged; Diderot simply forgot about the idea. However, some months later, a publisher named Le Breton contacted me concerning his plan for a French translation of Ephraim Chambers' *Cyclopaedia*. He proposed in fact to enlarge and extend the work, and wanted technical assistance with the scientific entries. I agreed to help, and also mentioned the name of Diderot, who was promptly enlisted as a translator. When the editor resigned from the project soon afterwards (following an argument with Le Breton), Diderot and I were appointed to replace him. We were now to be co-editors of the *Encyclopédie*.

We could see at once the immense possibilities; a project extending far beyond Le Breton's original proposal. The series of volumes as we conceived them were to be a grand survey of the whole of human understanding and achievement, beginning with a Preliminary Discourse which would outline the way in which our vast range of subject matter could be organised and classified. Diderot and I discussed the problem.

"Remember," said Diderot, "that philosophy can be divided into three parts."

"Yes," I replied; "Rousseau, D'Alembert and Diderot!"

"No, what about Music, Science and Poetry?"

"We want to embrace far more than these alone," I said. "The *Encyclopédie* takes in everything, the entire circle of knowledge, as the Greek word implies."

"Or tree of knowledge, as Bacon has it."

"Very well then," I said, "what are the first branches of the tree? What are the faculties from which all knowledge stems? I shall tell you: they are Memory, Reason and Imagination."

"Wonderful!"

"Memory leads to history in all its forms; the history of human civilisation, and also of the natural world. Reason is embodied in philosophy, which in its highest form is mathematics, and which includes all of science. On the third branch, Imagination, we find Poetry in all its varieties; drama, opera and romance."

"What about painting?"

"As a form of art it belongs with Imagination."

"Where then do we put crafts and industry? How does my father's cutlery business fit into your scheme?"

"I suppose I might place it on a sub-branch of History; the history of the uses of natural materials."

Diderot thought the idea brilliant. The Prospectus to the *Encyclopédie* would include a table in which the whole of the classification would be laid out.

From the very beginning, the subject and scale of our venture made it an object of interest not only to all people of culture and education, but also to the state. More than five years would pass before the publication of the first volume, and during that period of tireless labour we would have to undergo all manner of harassments. But before then I had already risen to become Permanent Secretary of the Academy, an appointment which owed something to the influence of a very powerful acquaintance who appeared in my dream, if I remember rightly, as some intractably divergent integral. This woman was the formidable Madame du Deffand. When I came to know her she was already past fifty and overcome by blindness, and there was little trace remaining of whatever charms she may once have held for the opposite sex (her husband left her after she was discovered in a scandalous affair). Nevertheless she still had a way of commanding and manipulating all around her which ensured that she always managed to get her own way.

Since the death of her estranged husband, she had been occupying a very grand suite of rooms on two floors of the Convent of St. Joseph, and it was here that I began to attend her salon, along with such friends and acquaintances as Montesquieu and Voltaire. Jean-Jacques also attended (having by now climbed quite considerably up the social ladder). This salon was regarded as the very heart of Parisian intellectual life in the middle years of the century. Invitation to it was a highly prized commodity; its withdrawal a grave punishment. Madame du Deffand, that great withered woman, would preside over everything; her recent loss of sight having done little to affect her spirits, other than to enhance her natural temper.

The great event took place every Thursday evening, when I would leave my lodgings at the house of dear Madame Rousseau (still I had not abandoned my foster mother, though I was in my thirties) and go to that luxurious apartment at the Convent. The society of Paris had other attractions also – on Wednesdays, for example, it was Madame Geoffrin who held court, and I would go to discuss philosophy with Saint-Lambert, Marmontel and the others. But it was Madame du Deffand (somewhat to the annoyance of the sober Madame Geoffrin) who attracted the brightest stars.

And it is here that my story (if not my dream) truly begins; for it was at the salon that I met the woman who was to consume more energy than I ever devoted to mathematics or to the *Encyclopédie,* and was to inspire in me both my greatest hopes and deepest sorrows. This woman was Madame du Deffand's companion, Mademoiselle de L'Espinasse.

Julie-Jeanne-Eléonore de L'Espinasse was born on the 9th of November 1732. She told me the birth took place during a violent thunderstorm – this fact strikes me as somehow appropriate. Even if the detail was another of her deceits, it is nevertheless one which I find agreeable.

So let us imagine the rain driving down upon the chateau of Avauges, and the intermittent rolls of thunder. Inside, the Comtesse d'Albon is attended to by the midwife, who patiently holds her hand, mops her brow, and hopes that they can get it all over with as quickly as possible.

At last! A girl.

The father was not present at the chateau of Avauges to witness the arrival into the world of his offspring. Comte Gaspard de Vichy was at his own home near Lyons, for already he had had enough of his affair with his own cousin, the unfortunate Comtesse.

I do not believe that she could ever have entertained the idea of maintaining any lasting relationship with Vichy, and no doubt the conception of a child was just another inconvenient accident (how familiar the story sounds!). Nevertheless, she would turn out to be rather fond of the infant, wiped clean now and crying heartily, which the midwife has placed beside her.

Her own husband the Comte d'Albon, in case you are wondering, has no part in this tale. He departed years earlier in search of new delights – the traditional sport of the aristocracy – leaving his wife to bring up their two children; a girl named Diane (who was already aged sixteen when Julie made her appearance), and a younger boy called Camille.

So now a third child has arrived to join them. It was, she said, during a thunderstorm. And she also told me she could remember the smile on her mother's face as she first took the new child to her breast. For the Comtesse had decided already that though the pregnancy may have been undesired, the child would not be. Did she perhaps see in those wandering day-old eyes some remnant of the cousin she still yearned for? I can only hope not, though the notion that Julie may have inherited something from him would explain much later on.

Those early days must have been a time of great happiness. Diane and Camille were too old to have played much part in Julie's early life, but from her mother she received a great deal of attention. I suppose the good woman had little else to distract her, in the chateau of Avauges. And the child soon proved to be unusually bright – she could learn songs after hearing them only once, and would make up new ones of her own. Her capacity for learning words (in Latin and Greek as well as French) was considered remarkable not only by her doting mother, but by her governess also. From the start, it was clear that this was no ordinary child. Julie herself later suggested to me that the electrical discharges from the thunderstorm may have energised her brain in some way, but I regard this as merely fanciful.

When she was seven, she met her father for the first time. Gaspard de Vichy returned to visit the chateau of Avauges, and took an instant dislike to the young girl who was presented to him. He saw her only as a symbol, a token of something he would rather forget. He would have liked to erase her completely.

The chateau, however, had other attractions for him. The Comtesse, his cousin, was by now rather too old to satisfy his tastes; Diane, on the other hand, was twenty three and quite handsome. Gaspard decided to marry her.

To take as a wife the daughter of one's former mistress was a step unusual even in those days, but Gaspard de Vichy was unusual in his total disregard both for convention and for the human feeling and natural morality which had brought those conventions into being. He saw something he liked, and he decided to have it. In any case, it was probably a relief to the Comtesse to have Diane off her hands – a difficult, spoiled child who somehow seemed to blame her mother for the absence of her natural father. The Comtesse's attempts over the years to win Diane's affections had only made the daughter resent her mother even more, and she resented also the young girl, Julie, whom the Comtesse showered with a devotion which was wholly natural and unforced. Pleased with her catch, Diane departed with Gaspard for his chateau at Chambron.

Nine years pass. Julie is now sixteen – a plain girl, but charming, intelligent, and quite without the affectations which might have infected her had she been brought up in the full heat of society. It is too much to ask that she will make an outstanding marriage, but she may at least achieve something adequate, and be well looked after. And this is, after all, the only hope for her – since there is no-one from whom she might inherit. Certainly not from the absent husband of the Comtesse, nor from Gaspard, who completely disowned her. But then, in 1748, the Comtesse d'Albon becomes gravely ill. She can see that there is no hope – all that matters is to make sure that somehow or other Julie will be provided for. She suggests a nunnery, but Julie resists; how could such a lively mind yield to the austerity of a convent? All is in vain – the most that the Comtesse can provide is a modest annuity which will stave off total poverty. And on her deathbed she gives Julie a key, telling her to go afterwards and look in the desk to which it belongs.

Out of pride or fear, or some twisted sense of duty, Julie gave the key to the Comtesse's executor. In the desk, there was a small fortune in cash, all of which went to Diane. And to Chambron also went Julie herself – there was nowhere else to go, and the Comte de Vichy (her father) had graciously offered to take her in as governess to the three children he now had by her half-sister Diane. Any other arrangement might have seemed like an acknowledgment of Julie's legitimate right to inherit part of his estate. And so she went to that dismal chateau outside Lyons, and her life there during the following five years was one of extreme misery. Had she been a servant her existence would have been easier. As it was, she lived in the conditions of a servant, but was constantly reminded by her father and half-sister of the enormous favour they had done her. Her only consolation was the children for whom she cared; Nicolas, Sophie and Abel.

Abel, the youngest, had the bright eyes and fair hair of Julie's mother, and a sweet and loving nature. Julie began to teach him to read, though he was not yet four years old. They sat together on the floor, Julie placed a piece of paper before him and wrote his name in large letters.

"Abel." She pointed. "Say it."

The child repeated his own name, and giggled. Julie said each letter in turn: A, B . . . In the following days she would continue this lesson, gradually adding other words so that within a few weeks he could recognise and read out several. One morning Diane came to see what she was doing. The other children were playing, Julie and Abel were on the floor.

"What sort of a lesson is this?" Diane asked sternly.

"Look Madame," Julie told her sister. "He's writing." Julie had cut up a number of pieces of paper, each of which bore a letter. Abel was arranging the letters as if trying to form words. Diane bent down to speak to her son.

"Very well, then, show me your name. Here's A." She put the piece in front of him, and he stared at it in silence. "Alright, what's next? Can't you find it?"

Julie could see fear and anxiety spreading across the little boy's face. His lip was dribbling.

"Don't bubble now," Diane said harshly, "show me the letter. Show me what a good teacher you have."

The other two children had stopped playing and watched nervously. Julie could not remain silent. "Madame, please, he hasn't had many lessons."

Diane snapped back at her, "Don't interfere! Do you think I don't know how to educate my own children?"

Julie stood up. "If you're angry with me then I would ask you not to take it out on little Abel. He's done nothing wrong."

For a moment Diane was speechless, her face reddened.

"How dare you presume to speak to me like that! I'll be the judge of what's right and wrong in this house. " She pulled Abel up by the arm, and he gave a squeal.

"Madame, you're hurting him."

With her free hand Diane slapped Julie's face. "I shall hurt whoever I please, and you will do exactly as you're told if you wish to retain the good favour and protection of Monsieur le Comte."

"Sister, I shall not stay here any longer." Julie left the room. She went downstairs and then out into the grounds of the dismal chateau, wandering in despair until she stopped to lean against a tree, where she wept. A convent would be the only possible escape; she would have to replace one kind of misery with another. When she went back inside she told Diane of her intentions, and it was agreed that arrangements would be made.

She would escape this fate, however. Next day word arrived that they were shortly to receive a visit from Madame du Deffand, who was the Comte's sister. Her salon was by this time already famous, but the blindness which would eventually become total had begun to take hold of her, and in a mood of depression she had decided to go to Chambron to rest. She arrived the following week in a handsome coach, along with a very large number of bags. Julie watched from an upstairs window as the grand woman ascended the front steps with a stick in one hand and a servant holding the other so as to guide her. The Comte tried to assist.

"Stop fussing brother, it's my eyes I'm losing, not my marbles. Just make sure they put all my luggage in the right place. And where's that skinny wife of yours?"

"I am here, Madame."

Madame du Deffand let go of the servant and brought her face close to Diane's, examining her with what sight she had. "Still haven't put on any weight then? Fatten her up, Gaspard, or she'll never last. Potatoes, Diane, lots of potatoes." Dogs were yapping, another servant was carrying Madame du Deffand's pets. "They probably eat better than your wife. Get a new cook, Diane. And lots of potatoes."

Later she had the children and their governess brought to see her. Madame du Deffand stared closely at Julie's face and figure. "Not a pretty one," she said bluntly. "That's good. Beauty should always be in its proper place. Do you read, girl?"

Julie told her it was her chief pleasure.

"In that case you shall read to me before I retire tonight. And you shall accompany me during my walk this afternoon."

Diane intervened, "But the children . . ."

"You shall look after the children, Diane. It won't kill you. And make sure you eat enough at dinner time, we don't want you fainting. There's nothing worse than women fainting all over the place, there seems to be a fashion for it among the young these days. One of my chairs was quite spoiled some weeks ago when a woman tried to fall upon it who had a rather healthier figure than you, Diane. Too many potatoes in her case. And such a lovely walnut chair."

In the afternoon, Madame du Deffand summoned Julie to escort her on her walk. They followed a path which Julie often took, and Madame du Deffand made her describe in detail everything which her weak eyes could not discern. For Julie it was an incalculable pleasure, to be able to give voice to all those impressions which she knew so well but had never shared with anyone.

During Madame du Deffand's visit, these walks became a treasured daily ritual. Then at night Julie would sit by her aunt's bedside, reading in a voice which Madame du Deffand praised for its clarity and melodiousness.

One evening Madame du Deffand summoned her a little earlier than usual. "Julie, we must talk. Sit down please." Julie obeyed.

"I know that you intend to go to a convent, and I can understand your wish to be away from Chambron. My brother is not an easy man to get along with, and given his unfortunate obligation to you it is hardly surprising that you should have received so much hostility from him and his wife. Your brother Camille still loves you, but he has a family of his own to look after and can't be expected to take you in. And marriage, of course, is out of the question.

"I'm being honest with you because I like you very much, Julie. You are clever but do not flaunt it, you can be witty when called upon, and you have an obedient spirit. This is all very much to your advantage. You don't want to enter a convent, you only want to be away from here, and during the last few days I have grown rather attached to your company and good services. I wish you to return with me to Paris."

Could anyone doubt the readiness with which Julie agreed? Madame du Deffand had already cleared the matter with her brother, having reassured him that there would be no threat to the family inheritance; Julie would go as her companion, not as a member of the family. Once the Vichys had it all in writing, they let her go.

And this was how Julie de L'Espinasse made her way to Paris; the town where she would find fame enough to outshine even the grand Madame du Deffand. Her lifestyle at the Convent of St. Joseph was a marked improvement on the privations of Chambron, though still it was an existence lived for the benefit of others rather than herself. At the salon she contributed to the atmosphere of wit and intelligent conversation, and for Madame du Deffand she provided invaluable assistance, waiting on her every need. Each night Julie would watch, over the pages of her book, the nodding head and drooping jaw of her aunt, and try to discern when it was that she was asleep, and Julie was free to go.

Madame du Deffand's apartment was famed for the tastefulness of its furnishings. The walls of the dining room were hung in yellow watered silk decorated with a pattern of small red bows. These red and yellow tones were reflected in the upholstery of the chairs, which were well positioned so as best to serve the needs of conversation. There were tables for piquet and écarté, and other tables were brought in as needed when food was served; dinner was at six and supper at eleven, and the fare was of a much more sumptuous kind than that served at Madame Geoffrin's (where spinach omelette recurred with celestial predictability). The conversation too was lighter and freer; the word "Enough" with which Madame Geoffrin would silence an unsuitable topic was never heard at Madame du Deffand's. And at her salon it was I who was the most prized jewel. I was thirty six, a celebrated figure – it was already two years since my Preliminary Discourse to the *Encyclopédie* had appeared and been hailed as a literary event. We had by now progressed as far as the letter D; I was working on my article *Différentiel*, and so it was the calculus which was foremost in my mind when I went to the salon.

"Monsieur d'Alembert, may I present my new companion, Mademoiselle de L'Espinasse."

A young woman stood before me – or rather stood over me, as she was rather tall. I kissed the hand of this plain young thing (she was twenty one), and my mind was still on Newton's beautiful theory.

"Mademoiselle, is this Aurora's gentle countenance I see before me?"

"You quote Boussard very well, monsieur."

"Have you seen the play?"

"No, but I have read it. Before coming to Paris I was able to learn a great many things, but to see very little."

"Once in Paris, most people unfortunately find the contrary to be the case. You will see many things, yet they will teach you nothing. I hope, mademoiselle, now you are here, that you will not spurn literature."

"Monsieur d'Alembert, once I have given my heart to something, then I can never abandon it."

"Clearly, mademoiselle, you are a most exceptional member of your sex."

Madame du Deffand had turned her blind face to talk to another group nearby. She returned now to interrupt us. "Julie! I hope you are not detaining Monsieur d'Alembert with idle talk. You are in the presence of a mind which must feed only on the rarest fruits of knowledge. Now girl, do please find for me Monsieur Turgot – I wish to chastise him about a very serious matter. Come along!"

During the course of the evening I was called upon by the company to perform as usual, to make witty remarks about absent persons, and impersonate their ways, and I was required to give my opinions on the latest performances at the Opera, and the question of whether the Italian manner was better than the French. This was a subject of heated debate at the time; the supporters of the French would sit near the King's box at the Opera, while the Italian party assembled beneath the Queen's, and from both groups a number of pamphlets had appeared. Along with Diderot and Rousseau I sided with the Italians, and yet I still felt much sympathy for the theories of Rameau, about which I had recently written a short book. After much criticism had been expressed against the abstract and theoretical quality of his work (so unlike the Italian style), I decided to say a few words in his defence:

"Rameau has stated, *When one considers the infinite relations the fine arts have to one another, is it not logical to conclude that they are governed by one and the same principle? And has one not today discovered and demonstrated that this principle is to be found in harmony?*

"For Rameau, harmony is the underlying rule of the cosmos. Not only does musical melody evolve from it, but nature itself is an embodiment of the concept. And what is harmony? It is a system of mathematical ratios. Or else, mathematics is the ideal expression of natural harmony. Rameau sees the cosmos through music, I see it through mathematics. These two visions amount to the same thing. We each regard nature as a consistent whole, something which can be reduced to a fundamental unity and simplicity, and hence comprehended. To understand the world, one must be in harmony with it."

While I spoke, I endeavoured (in accordance with the laws of rhetoric) not to address my words to any one person in particular, but rather to speak to all in equal measure. And yet I found myself unavoidably seeking out the face of Mademoiselle de L'Espinasse, who was seated in a corner, some distance apart from the main gathering. In mid-sentence, our eyes connected momentarily, and the sensation was strangely delightful. As I continued to speak, it seemed to me as if the words which issued from my lips bore no relation to those which began to pass through my thoughts:

"I imagine a cosmic dance of mind. The three mental faculties – Memory, Reason and Imagination – step together with perfect balance and symmetry, and the music which accompanies them is the harmony of the spheres. One of our composers could even try to write a suite along these lines; three contrasting movements, each evoking a different facet of our understanding, and forming a consistent and satisfying whole."

When the company laughed, she paused before joining in, her face frozen almost as if in embarrassment or expectation. What was the meaning of the expression she bore, which I could only glimpse so fleetingly? Was she listening to the words which I myself barely heeded, or was her mind perhaps wandering towards that same uncertain destination which had begun so irresistibly to attract my own thoughts?

"The principle of harmony; what a deliciously seductive idea! If only human affairs could obey the same rules which govern a piece of music or a mathematical equation! If only our own lives could be comprehended in terms of the just balance of parts, the equilibrium of opposing forces. Then the soul which is most at peace would be the one whose heart, freed from any turbulence which might disturb it, could beat with the steady rhythm of cosmic unity. And what more perfect form of friendship could there be than that silent harmony, unspoken yet profound, which might exist between two people whose hearts resonate together as one?"

She had lowered her face. Had my words impressed her, or did she find them merely ridiculous? Even after I finished speaking, and another guest took the floor, I still lacked the courage to go and make conversation with her; nor did she look again in my direction, so that I might be able properly to assess the opinion of me which her face may have betrayed. For the rest of the evening there was no further contact between us and I was left with a sense of uneasiness, a feeling I had never known before, and which refused to yield to any reduction or analysis in terms of former experience. Had my performance been a good one, or was I in fact the dullest of men, whom my companions merely flattered, while alone amongst them it was the newcomer who could see through the sham? And what sort of a woman was she; how might I catalogue or classify her qualities, so as to comprehend her reaction? My first encounter with her had been a frustrating one, but it was an experience which curiosity made me long to repeat. She posed for me a problem as interesting as the calculus onto which I lowered my head once more, after I had returned to my lodgings and kissed my maman good night.

Julie de L'Espinasse to Nicolas, Sophie and Abel de Vichy.
April 14 1753

You see, my little ones? Your old governess has not forgotten you. I hope that you are still applying yourself well to your lessons now that I am no longer there at Chambron to teach you. I trust that you will remain good children, and continue to do everything which your father the Comte instructs.

Life in Paris is very different – so busy and noisy! I really think you would not like it; you are all too fond of the fields, and the games you can play there. In Paris there is hardly a blade of grass that is longer than your thumb – not a good place to play.

Madame du Deffand's apartment is quite the grandest thing I have ever seen. There are so many mirrors! And in the evening when all the many candles have been lit, everything sparkles magnificently. The floor is very slippery though, since it is so well polished, and therefore everyone walks in a very slow manner which looks almost comical. I am sure that many of them have never once run in all their life, and would not know how to. God forbid there should be a fire!

Even my own rooms are quite sumptuous, such is the

kindness which Madame du Deffand has bestowed upon me. My apartment, though connected to hers, has its own entrance, so that when I am there I can feel that it is all my own. She really is a most generous soul – how sad it is that one who delights so much in splendour and spectacle should be chosen to lose the use of her eyes. It is indeed true that God rewards his people in strange ways, for she is certainly a most devout woman, and is always at great pains when I take her to Mass that I should place her at the correct seat, where she may be seen by many and thus provide a worthy example of Christian humility. And when she lies awake at night, unable to find rest, and calls out for me to comfort her, it is always some text of the most elevated kind which she asks me to read for her, such as de Lussy's stirring *Samson*.

She is truly a remarkable being, as I am sure you realise. But there are also many other fine examples here from whom I can gain the most valuable instruction – at the salon of Madame du Deffand, I am able to listen to the words of the most eminent men in Paris. What better schoolroom could there be than this? To hear the eloquence of the President Hénault, the Abbé Bon or Monsieur Turgot – this is worth more than burying one's head in a thousand silent books. How much there is yet for me to learn!

Madame du Deffand is particularly fond of Monsieur d'Alembert, who is well known for his work on the *Encyclopédie*. And truly, his knowledge is of a kind which seems to embrace every area of the arts and sciences. There is no topic on which he cannot converse, whether it is the theatre, or painting, or the most abstract philosophy. One would never imagine that such a versatile mind could live within so comical a figure! He is very short and slightly built, almost as if made of wire, while his speech is shrill and rapid as if he were perhaps rather nervous – though this cannot be the case, since he has such a fund of anecdote that he could never be lost for words. This excitability may be due on the contrary to the excessive energy of his brain. His face, which is neither very fine nor very ugly, is small and round, with a nose which is rather turned up, and he has about him a look which seems almost mischievous – as if he is never far from laughter. And in his discourse he is highly amusing, though in a way which can sometimes seem quite harsh. I cannot tell whether he is a naturally light person who feels the need to present himself seriously, or else a very earnest man who wins applause through a wit whose shallowness is perhaps unworthy of him. In any case, he is clearly a well-loved figure at the salon, and his comments are waited upon by all present.

He is also a very tactful man, and this is perhaps one quality which endears him to his friends. When I was first introduced to him, he compared me most sweetly to Aurora, and in my effort to be sophisticated I picked him up on his erudite quotation from Boussard. In fact (as it occurred to me almost immediately afterwards, and I checked later), the line is from Joliot's *Pyrrhus*. But Monsieur d'Alembert said nothing of it, asking only if I had seen the play. How kind and thoughtful of him, to have passed over my foolishness in silence. I only hope that he has not been left with a bad impression of me. Throughout the rest of the evening I felt most anxious about my grave error, and wondered if I should say something to him about it, though when I watched him speak to the assembled company he seemed to ignore me and to have forgotten all about the matter. I expect it was all too trivial for him to trouble himself over it – how silly of me even to mention it to you. I am very sensitive at this early and crucial stage that I should not make a poor impression here.

But I must not bore you, my dear children, with these silly things. The food here in Paris is quite astonishing – there are sweets such as you could never imagine. One day you shall come and see it all for yourself, if you are good and study well. Then I shall be able to introduce you to all these famous people I am telling you about. I am sure that when you are a little older you shall all make a most handsome spectacle here, and win many hearts, for there is none in Paris as lovely as you, my little ones.

Now I hear a cry – it is Madame du Deffand calling out to

me. I must go and read to her for a while, and so I bid you farewell. Remember me in your prayers.

A noise wakens me. Was it a new dream which passed before me, or else another fragment of that endless unrolling tapestry, the dream (or treatise) which is my life? I try to recall Julie, how did she appear in that treatise? As a most innocent looking equation, whose solution would however take many years to find. I saw her (in that moment when my head dropped) as I had first seen her at the salon – still little more than a child, and wholly free of the mannerisms of society. Her arrival at the Convent of St. Joseph was like a breeze of fresh air in that stifling place.

And so I began to make my visits there with a new enthusiasm; my performances (though naturally I would not admit it) were made principally for her benefit. Always when I spoke I would try to be sure that I was placed so that she could hear me, and all the while I would discreetly watch her reaction. You might say that I was in love.

But I prefer a view of the world which does not include such metaphysical concepts. What is love, other than a certain kind of behaviour? To say that I felt some particular sensation means nothing, since that sensation has left no spark or light in my memory which I can now rekindle. It is impossible for me to imagine now what it was that I must have felt, or what any person feels when he is gripped by such madness. I can merely note the strange deeds into which people are led by it. And if I consider the behaviour which denotes our idea of love, I see only a system of rules and signs which are quite without logic. The gestures by which we know two people to be in love, how might these have come into being? Is it all no more than some kind of language, learned through the imitation of our elders, whose every syllable is in fact wholly arbitrary, and determined only by convention?

My behaviour in those days, thirty years ago, might be labelled as "love," but what would such a label tell us? It would make it no easier for me to recreate within myself the feelings I had; a feat which is like trying to imagine ravenous hunger after the most satisfying meal. My actions at that time can only be attributed to delusion, and a state of belief which was wholly unfounded in observation. And this perhaps, is the essence of love; that it is a kind of faith, which is no more justified or explicable than any other superstition.

I shall not attempt to analyse the form which my sentiments took in those days; they had no place in my dream except perhaps as a kind of footnote, where they were dismissed as being nothing more than a hindrance to comprehension. Rather, let me proceed in recalling the historical facts.

Work on the *Encyclopédie* was continuing, and so was the controversy surrounding it. My enemies found fresh ammunition in 1756, when France went to war with Prussia, since I was by then in receipt of a pension from Frederick the Great in recognition of my achievements. More than twelve years had passed since my first meeting with Diderot, and it was six years since the publication of the Prospectus to the *Encyclopédie* which had announced our great scheme to the world. Now we were preparing Volume Seven, and both Diderot and I felt sure it would be the finest yet.

Diderot had acquired fame, but not wealth. His latest home (following numerous moves) was in the Rue Taranne, on the fourth floor of a building mostly occupied by poor working families. It was not a place I cared to visit, but Diderot would still sometimes entice me there. Once when I came I found Madame Diderot making soup which she then ordered her tiny daughter to take upstairs to a sick neighbour, though there was hardly enough to feed her own family. Diderot's appearance these days was more respectable (though he still went without a wig), but his home continued to maintain an indefinable atmosphere of criminality. When I arrived I saw evidence of a recently departed visitor who was, I guessed, the fugitive de Ville.

Diderot wanted me to look at an article he had received concerning the theory of probability. The article was nonsense, the ramblings of an uninstructed amateur (who would subsequently pester me on several occasions to publish his work), and since we still had not passed F it would be some time before I would need to consider the subject at all. So Diderot then began to tell me of the trouble he was having with Rousseau.

"It's impossible to say a single word without him taking offence," Diderot complained. I already knew this, of course. "He's proposing to go and live in some hut that Madame d'Epinay has had done up for him." Diderot threw up his hands. "Have you ever heard anything so bloody stupid in all your life? How can you be a philosopher and live like a savage? And will I still get all the musical articles I need from him? Yes, and while we're on the subject, what about that piece you were meant to be doing on fluxions – be quiet Angélique!" His daughter was at his side holding an empty soup bowl and trying to say something to him. When he raised his voice she shrank back, looking as if she might be close to tears.

"Perhaps I'd better go," I told him, getting up. "You'll have the article soon, I promise."

Diderot softened. "Jean, please." He came and put his broad hands on my shoulders and made me sit down. "I'm an impatient man, I know it. But at least I'm aware of my faults, which is better than many people. Yes, I'm flawed, but you're my friend Jean, and you know how much I need you. Let's have a drink."

"No, please," I said, "I must keep my head clear. I have a calculation to do later." I would also be attending Madame du Deffand's salon, and did not wish to offend Julie with any sign of intoxication.

Diderot uncorked a bottle and called to his wife to bring two glasses, which she set down on the table before us. She seemed to scowl at me as she left the room, taking the little daughter with her.

"This *Encyclopédie* will kill us all," Diderot growled, pouring himself a glass of wine. "Le Breton has invited me to go to his summer house for a rest. I'll be able to write there. I need to move away from philosophy for a while; I'd like to try drama."

Diderot's philosophy had never impressed me. One of his most recent books was an obscure series of ruminations on obstetrics, magnetism and steel-making (among other topics), the only purpose of which was for its author to demonstrate his intellectual virtuosity. He had a large talent, to be sure, but it was not one which included the ability to present a sustained argument systematically. Diderot had even asserted that mathematics was a dead subject, limited in the scope of its application, and had merely laughed at my objections. It had not occurred to him that his views might be hurtful to me, nor that he could possibly have been mistaken.

Over the years I had come to realise that while Diderot was brilliant at organising and focussing the efforts of others so as to achieve magnificent results, he did this through a form of emotional manipulation which really amounted to little more than bullying. He made everyone around him want to be his friend, since they feared being his enemy. And although he demanded total loyalty from his followers, he showed them little in return, gladly trampling on their feelings if this was what his "philosophy" dictated.

"You're looking at me so darkly, Jean." Diderot raised the glass again to his lips. "Tell me, what shall we do about Jean-Jacques?"

"You're the diplomat amongst us, Denis. You know how to say the right thing."

He prickled. "Are you suggesting that I am insincere?"

Of course not, I told him.

"If I seem so," he continued, "then it is only through consideration of others' feelings. I cannot be judged by anyone who doesn't know all the inner pressures I have to balance. It's like . . . it's like one of your dynamical systems, subject to so many external forces and internal constraints but, you know, all the while equivalent to a static – Angélique!"

The little girl, having re-entered the room unnoticed by either of us, had pulled over a small card table, bringing it crashing to the floor.

"You stupid child!" Diderot had risen and looked as if he might give her a thrashing, until his wife came and intervened.

I stood up. "Goodbye, Denis." He looked at me with an expression of helplessness, as if appalled by his own fury at the little girl whom Madame Diderot had led crying from the room.

"Forgive me," he said, close to tears himself. He asked me to stay longer, but I wanted only to escape from the tense atmosphere of the place. It was clear to me that the strain of work was driving Diderot to the verge of collapse.

I too needed to escape from Paris and its pressures, and so I was glad some weeks later to receive an invitation from Voltaire, exiled in Geneva, who had been contributing articles to the *Encyclopédie* for the last three years. He had been desperate to join our enterprise, and we tried to give him topics which would not be too controversial. He knew that an article on Geneva would be needed for the forthcoming volume, and suggested that I visit him so as to gather material.

The great man, a little shaky on his legs after an illness (he was sixty years old), greeted me on my arrival. "Ah, Monsieur d'Alembert, you have found me! You have discovered my hermitage, my Alpine cave."

His place was actually quite comfortable. I knew Voltaire; exaggeration was an essential feature of his view of the world. He was looking comparatively well, and had a good appetite when we dined together.

"Geneva has progressed enormously while I have been here," he told me. "The dark mantle of Calvinism is being cast off, gradually but decisively. I promise it won't be long before these backward people become part of the enlightened world."

He asked me for news of Madame du Deffand, and I extended her greetings to him. Their correspondence was at that time infrequent, but she was one of his oldest and most valued friends, despite their physical separation. "Are her eyes any better?"

Alas, I told him, the contrary was the case. She was rapidly descending into total blindness, as she had feared. Despite the private anguish this no doubt caused, she remained at great pains to present to the world a carefree image.

Voltaire said, "I hear her companion has made quite a stir at the salon. They say Mademoiselle de L'Espinasse is as much of an attraction as the hostess herself."

It was true that Julie's wit and conversation had enervated proceedings immensely. There would be two corners; in Madame du Deffand's the talk was merely social, while in Julie's it was of philosophy and politics. New guests had been attracted, and for foreign visitors the salon was essential.

"I dare say Madame du Deffand must find it a little unnerving to find herself upstaged by her protégée," Voltaire continued. "I'm also of the older generation, I know what it is to hanker for the old way of doing things, and to view the young with dismay, since they carry so nonchalantly the golden prize of which the years have robbed one. But time must pass." There was a look of sadness in his eyes. "And I hear that Mademoiselle de L'Espinasse's impact has been more than purely intellectual."

"What do you mean?"

"Her Olympian wisdom has melted a few hearts. Your own, perhaps?"

I blushed and denied it.

"I believe that others have found it harder to resist her lofty charms. This Englishman Taaffe, for example."

"What gossip is this?" John Taaffe had been a recent arrival at the salon; he liked to associate himself with the *philosophes*, and had clearly found great pleasure in Julie's conversation. But the idea that there might be any liaison between them could be no more than malicious rumour.

Voltaire raised his eyebrows and looked towards the ceiling, where a fly was buzzing. "Madame du Deffand had to write to him to make him call it off, and I hear that Mademoiselle de L'Espinasse responded by swallowing some opium in a fit of pique."

I was furious. "Who has been telling you such things?

How dare they insult the name of Mademoiselle de L'Espinasse in this way?"

Voltaire's eyes still followed the circling insect, and he smiled cynically. "I am like an old spider, Monsieur d'Alembert. From where I sit I feel the slightest tremor in every corner of my web."

"In this case I believe your scandalmongers are comically mistaken. Mademoiselle de L'Espinasse was unwell recently, but it was the result of a fever brought on by the excessive demands of her protectress."

Certainly Julie's life was an exhausting one, especially since Madame du Deffand's blindness had been having a strange effect on her sleeping habits. Always an uneasy sleeper, her insensitivity to daylight had made her hours of rest more and more irregular; she would remain awake through the night, then sleep from early morning until six o'clock in the evening. Julie (who was still called upon to entertain Madame du Deffand by reading to her) had therefore to try and find rest during the day, rising at five to prepare for the evening's activities. This unnatural schedule was taking its toll on the sensitive Julie, and I had no difficulty in discounting Voltaire's allegations. It was only years later that I discovered that what he said was perfectly true, and that he had learned it all from Madame du Deffand herself. These two ageing figures – one blind, the other far removed from the scene of events – saw and knew far more than I did.

Voltaire tactfully changed the subject. "Tell me about the theatre in Paris. As you know, such wholesome entertainment is forbidden here by the Calvinists, who dislike anything which might move men to emotions other than mute piety."

I stayed with Voltaire for three weeks. He introduced me to local society and educated me in Genevan manners and culture, providing me with a written exposition of the constitution of the republic. Our lively debates were a spectacle which drew much interest and admiration; in our private conversations no more mention was made of Julie de L'Espinasse.

I returned to Paris and began my article on Geneva, laden with material. Voltaire had already suggested the topics which I ought to cover, and the task of writing was an easy one. I forgot all about the rumours I had heard concerning Julie, having totally dismissed them, and continued to delight in the pleasure of her company each time I visited the Convent of St. Joseph. All were eager to hear about Voltaire, and Julie showed a particular interest. On the pretext of telling her about my visit, I spoke to her privately, and was soon able to bring up the matter which concerned me.

"You have not been in the best of health, Julie. I am concerned that you are over-exerting yourself."

She agreed that the last few months had been difficult for her. "Madame du Deffand is a demanding woman, and allows me little time which I can truly call my own."

"Your life has always been devoted to giving happiness to others," I said.

"Yes, if only I could find some for myself also! How I envy you men, who can lead independent lives and pursue your dreams and inspiration to the full. My only hour of freedom is the one which I make for myself before Madame du Deffand wakes up each evening. That hour is so precious to me, it is a time when I can feel truly myself." She looked at me with a gleam in her eye. "Will you visit me, before the beginning of the salon next week? Come to my rooms at five o'clock; we shall have an hour of freedom before the great Polyphemus awakens."

I looked forward to the meeting with a sense of anticipation which was almost unbearable. But when I arrived the following week and went to Julie's suite I found Turgot and Marmontel there already. I had not been alone in being invited, and my heart sank at the realisation that the favour I had been granted was not unique. "Dearest friends," she said when she entered the room to greet us, "Let us talk freely, while we may."

She felt no need to hide her dislike of Madame du Deffand's tyrannous regime, and we three guests could all easily imagine how the formidable woman dealt with those who depended on her favour. We joked about her like naughty schoolchildren, then when the hour drew to an end we all got up and made our way to Madame du Deffand's dining room, where we appeared without mentioning the secret rendezvous we had shared. These surreptitious meetings, Julie's own alternative salon, would continue for the next seven years. Chastellux would attend, and Condorcet; soon Julie's private rooms became the meeting place for all the best intellectuals, who would then show up an hour later at the official salon. Only Madame du Deffand remained ignorant of this convenient arrangement.

In October 1757, Volume Seven of the *Encyclopédie* was published, and the article on Geneva caused an immediate storm. I had a meeting with Diderot, who was as harassed as ever.

"What were you playing at?" He wrung his hands in despair.

"Didn't you read the article in proof? You could have stopped it then if you didn't like it."

"All this about the theatre, and the narrow-mindedness of the Calvinists. You even have bad words for Calvin himself!"

"Do you disagree with any of it?" I asked.

"Of course not, but that's hardly the point. Your attack on the pastors looks set to start a diplomatic crisis. This is the last thing we need." He buried his head in his hands, and I heard him say, "Thank God I had nothing to do with it."

"What do you mean by that?"

Diderot looked as if he hadn't slept. "You got us into this mess, you're going to have to get us out. The pastors want an apology and a retraction."

"That's quite out of the question."

Diderot stood up and began to pace about. "Come on, Jean, you got everything in the article from Voltaire, he set you up."

I told him this was quite untrue.

"Do you really give a damn about Geneva? Apologise and let's have done with it, what harm is there in that? Keep the idiots happy."

"I'm afraid I can't treat the truth quite so flippantly as you."

"Ah, forgive me," there was a distinct note of sarcasm in Diderot's voice. "This is a matter of principle is it?"

At that moment I felt as much hostility towards him as I did towards those who disliked my article. "I will not retract. Sort it out any way you like, I hereby resign at once from the *Encyclopédie*."

I walked out, leaving Diderot stunned and speechless. When Voltaire heard what was going on he wrote to support me, saying that I must never give in over the article. Diderot meanwhile presumed to send apologies to the Genevans on my behalf, which only made me all the more resolute in rebutting his attempts to make me withdraw my resignation. After several months I agreed to maintain some control over the scientific and mathematical articles, but otherwise my involvement was at an end, as was my relationship with Diderot. Rousseau was also lost. The article on Geneva (his birthplace) provoked him to write a denunciation which turned into an attack on my character. I felt weary and embattled.

I was forty years old, famous and as much loved by some as I was reviled by others (for such is the nature of fame). I realised that it all meant nothing to me, that I lived only for the hour when I would leave the house of my foster mother and go to see Julie, whose secret salon grew and blossomed, while with Madame du Deffand my relations became progressively more sour (I had even admitted as much in my correspondence with her friend Voltaire). She knew that I preferred Julie's company to her own, and made no secret of her resentment. A turning point came when I sent word one day that I would be unable to attend the salon. I was working on a calculation of planetary orbits which proved in fact to be much more straightforward than I had anticipated. I solved it easily, felt highly satisfied, and decided to go to the Convent of St. Joseph after all, since it was still not late.

It was my custom always to arrive unannounced. I found proceedings well underway; a circle had formed, the blind old woman sat while Turgot read out a letter which I soon realised was a copy of one which Madame du Deffand must have sent (or intended to send) to Voltaire. Turgot (and the rest of the company) clearly had not noticed my arrival.

"You say that D'Alembert has described me as an old whore; I find this amusing and also a revelation. That D'Alembert has any experience of whores is, if anything, reassuring; since like most people I had assumed him to have no interest in any organ other than the brain, and believed him moreover to be incapable of finding any physical pleasure with the opposite sex. Now that I know he has healthy tastes after all I can suggest any number of women who might educate him further; women who would take pleasure in his singular physique and feminine voice."

Julie saw me as I turned to leave. Her face was pained and she was blushing deeply with anger and embarrassment. She would act as mediator in achieving a reconciliation between Madame du Deffand and myself, but I would no longer feel any allegiance to the woman who had once been so useful in furthering my career.

The salon continued uneasily until 1764, when Madame du Deffand finally found out about Julie's secret receptions. She already had enough work on her hands maintaining her superiority over Madame Geoffrin; to have to deal with her own niece as well was intolerable. Julie would have to go.

The salon split in two, as each member chose for Julie or for Madame du Deffand. My choice was easy, and many others followed, including people whom Madame du Deffand had counted as her most loyal allies. It must certainly have been a bitter blow to the old woman, who had never questioned the high esteem in which she was held by all around her, and yet now so many of them were deserting her.

But her star had set, and now it was Julie's turn to rise as the greatest hostess in Paris. There were of course some practical difficulties to be overcome; principally that she had no money, and nowhere to live. Madame Geoffrin was only too pleased to come to her aid; out of genuine affection, as well as the desire to settle old scores with her rival. She granted Julie a sizeable annuity, and helped set her up in an apartment on the Rue de Bellechasse, not far from the Convent of St. Joseph. There was no shortage of assistance from other quarters; the Duchesse de Luxembourg provided furniture, and from all her many friends came gifts of money or household goods. I also gave all the help I could, and in fact it would not be long before I myself took up residence in the Rue de Bellechasse.

The upheaval in Julie's life had its effect on her delicate health, and soon after she had moved to her new home I received word that she had fallen ill. I went at once to see her, and found her unconscious in her bed, her face streaked with feverish sweat. She had smallpox.

"My dearest Julie!" I sat down beside her and dismissed the servant, since I did not want anyone else to see the distress which the terrible sight caused me. I held her hand for the first time, though already I had been in love with her for more than a decade. At last she opened her eyes.

"Monsieur d'Alembert, you came! I was hoping you would."

"How could I do otherwise; do you think I would carry on with my work when I knew that you were all alone without anyone to talk to?"

"But your work is very important, Monsieur d'Alembert; I must not keep you from it. Tell me what it is you are studying."

"Oh, let us not concern ourselves now with mathematics."

"Please, Monsieur d'Alembert. I want to hear you speak, while I try to rest. Tell me about this problem which you find so interesting."

I began to explain my work, and she closed her eyes. She slept for an hour or more, while I sat beside her in silence. Then suddenly, without warning and with her eyes still closed as if in sleep, she cried out.

"Ah, Abel!"

"Julie, what is it?"

"So you have come to see me – what a fine young man you have grown into!"

"Julie, you are delirious . . ."

"Let me show you all the mirrors – you see how splendid it is? But beware of the great blind ogre who lives here . . ."

"Please, wake up – these are only dreams."

"She will snap off your head if she finds you here, Abel – run and hide over there. Look, everyone is arriving . . . but where is Monsieur d'Alembert?"

"I am here, Julie, beside you."

"I cannot see him anywhere. Where is my friend? I do so long for him to make me laugh, for there is no-one else as witty as he."

"Julie, you must stir yourself. It is I, your friend."

"What voice is that? Is it the mirror which is talking to me? How can a mirror speak, unless the one who gives it its reflection should decide to allow it? What do you wish to say to me, mirror?"

"Julie, can you hear me?"

"Indeed mirror, I can – now will you tell me where Monsieur d'Alembert might be?"

"He is at your side, and wishes you to rest."

"I cannot rest until I find him. Is there anything else you wish to tell me, mirror?"

She could hear me, but could not comprehend who it was who spoke. Under these strange conditions I found at last a courage which had failed me for years.

"Julie, Monsieur d'Alembert loves you."

"And I love him most dearly also, since he is my friend."

"I mean, Monsieur d'Alembert is in love with you, and would give his own life for you."

"What nonsense, mirror! To be in love – what does this mean? Nothing more than a certain arrangement of bodily humours – has Monsieur d'Alembert not told you this himself? Where is he?"

"But love is more than that – it is a constant hunger . . ."

"And hunger is nothing more than the reaction of the nerves in the stomach to a lack of food. Could we not

73

imagine a machine which is capable of hunger? We might construct it in such a way that it has a bladder or sack into which it passes food for digestion, and instructs itself to repeat this action whenever the bladder becomes empty. Would we not then say that the machine feels hunger?"

"But Julie, it could not feel as I do . . ."

"Can you be sure of that, mirror? You yourself, after all, consist of nothing more than my reflection. If I pinch my cheek, do you then feel my pain or your own?"

"Your pain, Julie, is also mine."

"So that if I am more able to tolerate suffering and you are less so, then when you feel my pain does this mean that you actually experience something greater – in which case how could it be said to be the pain belonging to me? Answer me that, mirror."

"Julie you are rambling, you are talking nonsense."

"I am merely telling you some of the wisdom I have learned from Monsieur d'Alembert. But where is he?"

"He is with you, Julie, always. Wherever you go, his love will follow you."

"What foolish notion is that, mirror? The idea that something can be both with me and not with me; that it can exist within a body and yet also beyond it – that it has material location without material substance . . ."

"I love you, Julie, and I would die for you."

"But if you were to die, mirror, would I not also have to follow? For a being cannot live without her own reflection. And as for love, I thought we had already dismissed this notion as an absurdity."

"There is nothing absurd in the most profound and indubitable of human emotions."

"Most profound? In what sense are some emotions deeper than others? And how do you doubt a feeling? Can I feel hungry, and yet be mistaken?"

"There is certainly no mistake in my feelings for you, Julie."

"You perplex me, mirror. You say that you are certain of something which appears to me to be a logical absurdity. In that case you must talk nonsense – and since you are nothing but my own reflection, then perhaps so do I."

"Julie, I wish only to know one thing. Do you think that you could ever find it within your heart to love Monsieur d'Alembert, as he loves you?"

But already she had lapsed back into the most profound sleep, in which she remained for a considerable time. At last she awoke.

"Monsieur d'Alembert – you are still here! How happy I am to see you. I believe I had a most strange dream, in which I heard your voice. Were you speaking to me?"

I trembled at her words, but tried to remain calm. "Can you remember anything of what you heard?"

"Something about an astronomical calculation you were performing – is that correct?"

I never told her about our unusual conversation. Every day I maintained my vigil at her bedside, but the nightmarish visions which had seized her did not return. Within a few weeks, she was restored to health, though the scars of smallpox would remain.

Julie was clearly touched by the efforts I had made to be near her during that difficult time. She sent word that she would like to speak with me, and when I saw her she gave me her thanks, and told me that I had demonstrated a friendship which she would always honour.

"There is another thing, Monsieur d'Alembert, which I should like to mention. I am aware that your lodgings with Madame Rousseau are not very spacious, and though you are clearly devoted to your foster mother, I wondered whether you had considered moving somewhere where you would be able to enjoy greater freedom to work, and would in addition be closer to the friend who needs your companionship so greatly? The floor above this apartment has become vacant, and I should like you to consider taking it."

Need I tell you my decision, or the joy with which it filled my heart? And so, at the age of forty eight, I finally left the home of my beloved foster mother who had shown me such unfailing devotion, and I entered into the gravest error of my life.

VI

D'Alembert gave a moan, but Justine knew that he was still asleep. When she had come to take the tray of food he had left untouched she saw that his arm no longer wrote, that his head was lowered onto the page, and that his work (which must have occupied him throughout the previous night) had exhausted him. Now she was squatting on the floor beside the desk on which his head rested, having read the manuscript she found piled there. She had read quickly, checking all the time that D'Alembert would not stir, and that Henri did not return unexpectedly early, but nothing had occurred to disturb her. The master's face looked peaceful, though his mouth was slightly open, and he whistled as he breathed. A trail of spittle ran from the corner of his mouth onto the half-written sheet beneath his cheek.

She heard a noise and gave a start. No, it wasn't D'Alembert, but a sound outside. It was someone at the door. She quickly put the manuscript back in its place, exactly as she had found it, then picked up the tray she had come to collect and hurried out. It couldn't be Henri, unless he'd locked himself out, but this was not the hour to receive visitors (even though none came, a proper time was appointed for them should they do so). Justine put away the unwanted food, straightened her cap and apron and went to the door. A stranger waited there.

"I wish to see Monsieur d'Alembert."

"I'm afraid, sir, that isn't possible. If you'd like to leave word . . ."

He had already entered, and was unbuttoning his coat. He carried a stick in one hand and a satchel in the other, the sort in which lawyers might carry documents.

"Sir, he's asleep . . ."

"I'll wait until he wakes up."

"I'm sure he won't receive you." The man sat down in the lobby. "If you'd like to wait through here you'll be more

76

comfortable, sir." Justine showed him to the drawing room.

"When was this room last used?" the visitor asked when he saw it.

Justine was surprised by the question. "I'm not exactly sure, sir."

"The covers on those card tables haven't been lifted in years."

"I do clean every day, sir."

"I mean that the folds on them are long untouched. Your master clearly has few callers." The stranger sat down on one of the armchairs, testing it before applying all his weight, as if afraid it might fall apart. "And do you know why he is such a recluse?"

Justine knew now that it was because of Julie; that she was the one who had broken his heart. "I couldn't say, sir."

The visitor stretched in his chair. "Your master thought himself the most brilliant man of his generation, yet all his work adds up to nothing. His calculations are erroneous. I believe he may know this to be the case, even if he will not admit it."

Justine felt uncomfortable in the stranger's presence. He had a glint in his eye which might equally well indicate genius or insanity. Henri was out, the master was asleep and in any case incapable of defending either himself or his servant. "I really think Monsieur d'Alembert won't see you today. If you'd like to leave your name I'm sure he will receive you tomorrow."

"Do you read?" He was gazing at the play of sunlight on the gilded decoration of the walls.

"Yes. Yes I do, sir."

"What do you read?"

Justine didn't know what to say. She thought of the library with its vast store of knowledge from which she would steal every crumb she could.

"Have you ever seen the *Encyclopédie*?" he asked her.

"No sir." The complete set of volumes had been among the books which Justine had moved to D'Alembert's study.

"That's good. I would hate to think that it had corrupted your innocent mind."

77

Justine was gradually edging towards the door of the drawing room.

"Well, young lady, will you tell me what you do read then? Romances, perhaps?"

She was confused. "I've read . . . *Émile* . . ."

"Rousseau. An Encyclopaedist."

"And . . . and *Candide.*"

"Even worse."

"And . . . *Lucille* . . . *Tristram Shandy* . . ."

"Bah."

"*Tales From Rreinnstadt* . . ."

He exploded. "Rreinnstadt! A piece of Encyclopaedic non-sense from beginning to end, which even seeks to ridicule my own work explicitly. Its authors are mischievous hoaxers, snivelling hacks; all they can produce is an imitation of the pseudo-philosophical style of Diderot, inspired by the classification system of D'Alembert. How is the museum of their mythical 'encyclopaedia-city' divided? Memory, Reason and Imagination! Bah!"

Justine was apologetic. "Please sir, I'm only an uneducated servant, and the books I've read all came from the master's library."

"Yes, your taste is necessarily dictated by his poor judgement. Don't you realise that he and his cronies have polluted the intellectual well-being of the entire continent? And the man is a charlatan, a fraud! He knows this, I'm sure. He thinks the universe can all be explained from a single principle, a single Great Fact from which everything else logically follows, and can be mathematically deduced. He said as much in that absurd Preliminary Discourse to the *Encyclopédie*. His so-called Principle is mere tautology, a meaningless definition. His physics is hollow, he knows this. He has hidden himself from the world so as to mask his shame."

Justine thought otherwise. She knew now that Julie de L'Espinasse was the one cause from which everything in D'Alembert's life had followed. Her love was the principle on which he had staked everything, and his faith had been betrayed. He had seen the very foundation of his existence shattered, and all that was left was worthless and without meaning.

"Sir, I must insist that the master won't see you today. He needs his rest."

The visitor opened the satchel on his lap. "I've brought something for him to read. Over the years I've sent letters, papers, whole books to him on many occasions, but he has chosen to ignore me. My work on probability means nothing to him. Long ago I demonstrated to him that the certainties on which his science is based are illusions, that the universe is governed by the laws of chance; laws which he barely understands, but which I have worked hard to elucidate. The manuscript I have brought today is merely another in a succession of texts which show that other universes exist outside his philosophy, beyond the arid reaches of the accursed *Encyclopédie*.

"I came upon the text at the Convent of St. Joseph, the place where D'Alembert wasted so much of his time at the salon of Madame du Deffand. The Convent is an admirable institution, it affords respectable accommodation to all manner of widows or single women, and their guests. Many years ago, in the comfortable apartment of Madame de Vassé, Charles Edward Stuart – the Young Pretender – spent three years of his exile, surrounded by a curious retinue, remnants of which still meet there to reminisce, long after the departure of their patron. It was from the son of one of those who escaped Scotland along with Charles that I obtained the manuscript which I now hold. It is by a man named Magnus Ferguson, and I find it most enlightening. D'Alembert will hate it, of course."

Justine was sure now that the visitor was mad and possibly dangerous. There was no way she could persuade him to leave. "You may have to wait a long time," she said. "Excuse me."

She returned to the study to see if D'Alembert was awake yet, but he was still lying across his desk. She felt safer staying here at his side, until Henri returned. Even if D'Alembert was too frail to be of help, his presence might at least act as a deterrent should the visitor think of trying to molest her.

There was no more of D'Alembert's manuscript to read except the part he was lying on. Instead Justine turned her attention to the pile of letters on the desk. A quick glance was enough to reveal to her that they were in many different hands, and the open boxes beside the desk, each neatly labelled, indicated that D'Alembert had in his possession not only letters addressed to or written by himself (he had retained drafts of those made by his own hand), but also Julie's correspondence to various recipients, and letters written by several other people. In fact, though Justine did not know it, D'Alembert had (during his first year of residence here) been assiduous in his compilation of material which enabled him to know the whole truth concerning the events which took place between his arrival at the Rue de Bellechasse in 1766, and Julie's premature death (at the age of forty four) ten years later. Letters had been returned, donated out of sympathy, by way of explanation and apology. The pile of correspondence arranged on D'Alembert's desk had been put in order by him, perhaps to help him in writing the continuation of his memoir, and it was these letters which Justine began to read, as she nervously waited for her husband to return.

VII

Louis Vassard to Claude Martigny.   *April 24 1770*

It may interest you to know that I have visited D'Alembert recently. He expends little energy these days on useful research, but devotes himself instead to the woman whom some say is his lover, Julie de L'Espinasse. Others assert that their relationship is strictly that of a mistress with her lapdog, even saying unkindly that Monsieur d'Alembert is physically incapable of having natural relations with the opposite sex. For the last four years, D'Alembert has occupied the floor above Mademoiselle de L'Espinasse's apartment, but he spends most of each day attending to the needs of his friend, for whom he acts as secretary. Since her correspondence is quite large, this is a task which keeps him permanently busy, and anyone who wishes to see D'Alembert must also pay their respects to the woman who rules his existence. When I called on him he was with her as usual, apparently trying to teach her the meaning of Newton's laws of motion.

D'Alembert explained it like this. Imagine a cloud of particles; isolated points, wandering aimlessly without any awareness of each other.

"You mean," she said, "like the crowds who mill about the market of St. Jacques?"

"If you like. Individual, unconnected entities floating around. What controls their movements?"

"In the case of the market, Monsieur d'Alembert, I suppose it is their wish to buy goods as cheaply as possible."

"Very well, but perhaps we should forget the market. If a particle is left alone to wander freely, how will it move?"

"How would people behave if they were free? That is a very dangerous question, Monsieur d'Alembert."

"Please, Julie, let us not get blown off course. Imagine a particle in space, utterly alone and uninfluenced. How might it behave?"

"I suppose it would go here and there, idly turning one way and then the other in search of some diversion. Would that not be a plausible way for someone to act if he were alone and isolated?"

"On the contrary, if a particle changes its direction, then it surely must have been pushed by some external impulse."

"But Monsieur d'Alembert, if a person who is alone and solitary should suddenly decide to change the course of his life, then must this impulse have come from some outside source, or could he not have reached such a decision for himself, unaided?"

"Julie please, you misunderstand. A particle which is not acted on in any way has no reason to change direction or alter its speed. It will carry on, along the same course and at the same rate, forever."

"So you are telling me that the natural instinct of the particle is to continue indefinitely, without there being anything to push it?"

"Precisely. This is Newton's First Law of Motion."

"Your physics is all a great mystery to me, Monsieur d'Alembert, and as far as I can see it is quite contrary to common sense. If a thing is moving then there must surely be some force or impulse which makes it move, or else it should be standing still. If you see a man running, then is this not because he has decided to put one foot in front of the other and propel himself at speed? And yet you tell me that according to Newton's law it is in that man's nature to continue on his journey forever, without the need of any effort whatsoever! Clearly, Monsieur Newton never had any idle servants to worry about, or else he might have reached a different conclusion on the subject."

"My dear Julie, you always make the same mistake of trying to reduce physics to everyday experience, when really the correct way to proceed is the other way round. All experience is reducible to physics."

"I find that very hard to believe, Monsieur d'Alembert. The idea that my life, and all my sensations, are nothing more than cold physics – what a detestable notion!"

"Allow me to continue with my explanation. If a particle is acted on, then its motion will change. If a particle is moving uniformly, then this implies that there can be no external force acting upon it."

"I'll take your word for it, Monsieur d'Alembert."

"Now, as you will readily agree, the world is not made of isolated particles but rather of matter which is composed of smaller units bound rigidly together: so-called atoms. Yet Newton told us only how to study the motion of ideal particles which have no size. In order to deal with rigid bodies, one must take account of the forces of constraint which hold the constituent particles in place."

"Monsieur d'Alembert, I am becoming confused . . ."

"And my Principle enables not only this problem to be dealt with, but the motion also of far more complicated systems such as flowing water, or the air. In fact, my Principle gives a simple law, from which all of Newton's theory can be rederived, as well as all forms of motion in the world. It is the most fundamental rule of nature."

"And a truly marvellous achievement, Monsieur d'Alembert, for which I and the whole world heartily congratulate you. But I do wish you would realise that no matter how hard you try, I shall never be able to understand your wonderful theories; they are as incomprehensible to me as the language of the Chinese."

"No, Julie – mathematics is the easiest of all knowledge to comprehend. If I want to learn Chinese, then I must patiently learn a system of rules and symbols which have been developed by that race over many thousands of years – a system which is, in fact, wholly arbitrary, and fashioned only by convention and the mutual agreement of all those who use it. But in mathematics there is nothing which is arbitrary. If no-one taught you the rules of mathematics then you could still, if you were patient enough, discover them all for yourself."

"Monsieur d'Alembert, now you flatter me too much! Do you think that I could have made all of your wonderful discoveries?"

"If I had not made them, then someone else would have. Mathematics is nothing more than a series of peaks waiting to be climbed. I pride myself only on my good fortune of having been first to the top of some of them. And anyone can learn to climb, with a little exercise and training."

This was the conversation which I listened to. How pitiful it was to see a once-great mind reduced to idle self-flattery, in the hope of winning a woman's favour!

Julie de L'Espinasse to the Comte de Mora.   *August 2 1770*

José, it is almost four years since we first met and my life became filled with joy. Yet this secret happiness continues to make my life unbearable. Each week I receive the usual guests at my salon, I make the usual comments to the same faces, who all grow old before my eyes. I am sick of it! I long only to tell them that I do not care for their obscure philosophy, their erudite jokes, their wit which is sharp yet has no warmth. And every day I must maintain my composure against the concerned enquiries of Monsieur d'Alembert, whose loyalty merely fills me with disgust at my own insincerity. He has been a faithful companion since he took up residence near me, not long before you and I first met. Indeed you must recall that it was Monsieur d'Alembert who brought you to my salon; it was he who first told me all about the fine young Spanish diplomat, only twenty two years of age, who nevertheless had such a wealth of experience behind him! And yet how little he knows of what has passed since then; how your frequent absences have been the cause of my every illness, and how each letter which he has conveyed has been another token of the love which both sustains and destroys me.

Your father will never approve of me as your wife, I accept this, and I understand why it has been necessary to continue in this clandestine manner. But will you always be ruled by your father? Must we wait until he departs from this life before we can be honest in our happiness? Today I counted your letters. There are more than a hundred of them, from the times when you have been in Madrid, or else away from Paris as you are now because of your health. I imagine this pile of letters growing deeper and deeper until one day we fade into dust, having never been able to live together as man and wife. I know that you want us to be married. Why can we not find a way?

My entire existence is a falsehood. Monsieur d'Alembert delivers your letters to me, and I tell him that they contain news of the opera, or a report on a new play. I give him my reply to send to you, and tell him that I speak of a book I have read, or of a striking costume, and as I tell these lies my heart feels like stone. I have become so very good at deceiving people.

José, I love you, and have done since the first moment I saw you. And yet I do not have the advantage of your youth and fine features. It is from a great distance in time that you view me, a woman so much older, so much plainer than those whom you could so easily find to please you. You have shown great kindness to me, such fondness over the years, but I am afraid that perhaps you do this out of sympathy, that to you I am a poor creature who deserves pity and sensitive treatment. Do not act out of pity, I pray you. I love you, and if you cannot love me equally in return then tell me now, and I shall dream of it no more. To show generosity out of pity would really be the greatest cruelty, it would only raise my hopes to even greater heights before sending them crashing to the ground. Can I be sure that this secrecy is not simply a way for you to hide your own doubts about me? Would your father really find my existence so shameful?

Forgive me, dearest José. The last few days have been an agony for me. Even though we are so often apart, I still cannot grow used to the pain of separation. I have thought of you constantly, I have tried to imagine what you might be doing, and the sweet sound of your voice in my mind has only brought me further distress. Three days ago Monsieur d'Alembert noticed my torpor and asked if I was unwell. He insisted so unremittingly that there may be some physical ailment requiring attention that I was forced to admit that I was troubled by my thoughts rather than by any bodily disorder. He wanted to know what could be the source of such anguish, and begged me to unburden myself. He even got down on his knee, took my hand and implored me to share my pain with him. I told him that a certain person was in my thoughts a great deal, and caused confusion in my mind.

Who is this person, D'Alembert asked me. Has he wronged you in any way? Oh no, I told him, on the contrary. He has been kind and gentle to me, and has shown the utmost generosity. Then why should you be troubled? said Monsieur d'Alembert.

I should have been more discreet in my reply, I should have realised that he might mistakenly believe that it was he to whom I was referring, but the turmoil in my heart affected my judgement. I fear, I said to him, that my friend may act only out of sympathy, and that he might not share the deep feelings which I hold.

D'Alembert squeezed my hand tenderly, did not speak, but rose and left the room before I could think what more to say. For him to believe that I am in love with him, or else to learn that I am in love with some other man; either case is equally to be avoided. I need Monsieur d'Alembert, he is my closest friend. And yet the love he feels for me, and of which I have been uncomfortably aware since he first took up residence here, is an irritation which I find myself increasingly unable to ignore. What was once a harmless affection has slowly grown to become an oppressive barrier between us. How can I avoid hurting him now?

Much as I long for it, José, I also fear the day when it will be announced that we are to marry. I am sure that in his heart Monsieur d'Alembert knows the truth, and that many of my friends suspect but do not condemn me for my actions. Yet still I wonder if they will turn away from me, as they once turned from Madame du Deffand. I see myself as an old woman, blind to the love they have shown me. I have lived for you, José, and you alone. I wish only to live for you. Yet surely you must see what a great risk this is, to make the happiness of one man the very centre of one's existence, to make it the single condition on which one's own happiness depends. For me, this is the only kind of love there can be, and yet I know that it has the power to engulf and destroy me.

Do not be cross with me. I know that you too have your secret burden, that you must look at the women whom your parents offer you and find some excuse, some reason for rejecting them. But what if one day they were to find one whom you would not choose to reject? How many more years must I wait in dread of this?

And while you must keep coming to Paris on the pretext of diplomatic business, but really so as to see me, your health continues to be damaged by the climate here and the poor air. We could live together in the warm south, bathed in sunlight, we could both be free and healthy. But as soon as you are well you will come back to Paris, we will resume our clandestine meetings, each of us filled with longing and frustration, until we both fall ill again and you leave once more to recover.

Ah José, why must life be such an endless torment?

D'Alembert to J. C. de la Haye.   *March 12 1771*

Your research shows a good understanding of the principles of mechanics as I have outlined them in my Treatise. Nevertheless, your treatment of the moving string wholly overlooks the important work which I have already done on this subject. You are right, a vibrating string has not only length, mass and tension but other qualities as well. It has a certain thickness which may vary with its length, it may have irregularities of manufacture. But these imperfections, while they may be of subtle interest to a musician, have no place in mathematical analysis. The mathematician must begin with a world which is perfect, reduced to its purest elements. Only once this world is fully understood can those other blemishes be introduced, which give the real world the character we know. If you wish to understand the movement of a vibrating string you must begin by considering one which has no thickness whatsoever – an impossibility, I agree, but an assumption which is essential in order that one might begin to comprehend the problem. Begin with a string which does not sag, one for which the pull of gravity is irrelevant. Begin with a string which is not plucked sharply at one end, but is set in motion most gently. You are not prepared to make these assumptions; you say that physics is useless if it speaks only of the ideal. I say that the world can only be understood once the ideal has been mastered. Otherwise, all that there is is chaos, incapable of reduction. As mathematicians, are we any worse than those poets who speak of the gods, and of the noble deeds of ideal men and women? If a poet portrayed the world as it really is, he would show one which is for the most part incomprehensible, and in which little happens which is memorable or of interest. The poet selects, he makes assumptions about the world, he presents those aspects of it which it is within his power to understand and portray, and hence he may convince his audience of some point which hitherto might have escaped them. This is also the task of the mathematician; to seek truth, and to discover wonder.

To understand fully one tiny fragment of the universe is surely far more uplifting than to view it as a whole and throw one's hands up in hopeless defeat, faced by such magnitude. Perhaps it is true that I understand very little, and that the world's complexity must forever be beyond my reach. I can only say that within the restricted field I have chosen to explore I have discovered something pure, something absolute and unshakeable. Whether these discoveries can be applied elsewhere I cannot say. It may indeed be the case that by knowing so much about so little I am in fact the most ignorant of men.

Julie de L'Espinasse to the Comte de Crillon.   December 18 1771

Yes, friend, you know my secret. And it seems that it is a secret known to many others apart from yourself. I love the Comte de Mora with a passion which consumes me, I am like a candle glowing and burning, which must eventually extinguish itself through the action of its own flame. This love will destroy me, I know it, but I am helpless to resist. Is this not the true meaning of love?

Now he is in Madrid again, and I am more alone than ever. The air in Paris oppresses me, as does the poor light. The city is a good place to live if one seeks endless distraction, if one is amused by trivialities and constant change. But if one wishes to study one's own soul, or to find peace within oneself, then the city is merely a source of irritation which magnifies every anxiety. It is a place filled with people who speak easily, though their hearts are empty. It is an orchestra of hollow instruments, each trying to outplay the other.

There are days when I wish that I could start my life over, begin again and do everything differently. I see a poor flower seller in the street and I long to change places with her. I read about a caravan crossing a distant desert and I imagine the scorching heat, sand blowing in my face, into my nostrils, clinging to my lips. I imagine the discomfort, and I yearn for it. I sit in the opera, trying to listen to the music while idle chatter flies between the rest of my companions, and I dream that it is I who stand upon the stage; a character of fiction existing only in the most noble song.

Are you not weary of hearing all of this? Do you not think I am quite mad?

D'Alembert to the Comte de Céreste.   *January 15 1772*

People have been saying unpleasant things which, if they concerned only myself, would mean nothing to me. But it has come to my notice that Diderot, whom you know well and over whom you have some influence, has written a piece in dialogue form in which he portrays my friend Mademoiselle de L'Espinasse in a manner which is inaccurate and scandalous. My own portrayal in his work is of no interest to me. He has not seen me in more than seven years and cannot claim to be able to represent either myself or Mademoiselle de L'Espinasse accurately. But to make a mockery of a woman who is of the highest moral stature and who is not in a position to defend herself is unforgivable. I urge you to speak with Diderot and see to it that he destroys the work.

The dialogue is set, I believe, during a time when I was ill and was nursed by Mademoiselle de L'Espinasse; an act of kindness on which she insisted, saying that she wished to reciprocate my own gesture of friendship during the time when she was stricken with smallpox. I am told furthermore that Diderot's dialogue supposes me to talk in my sleep, and to say all manner of outrageous things. I cannot imagine where he might have found such an absurd idea for a piece of so-called literature. Whatever ridicule he may seek to shower on me is of no importance, but I am told that these supposed utterances of mine imply an improper relationship between myself and Mademoiselle de L'Espinasse. On behalf of the friend whom I have known for almost twenty years, and served for more than five, let me say that this allegation shocks and wounds me, since it must cause so much grief to her.

I have not spoken to Mademoiselle de L'Espinasse about this delicate matter, but I believe that she has been told of it. Do not expect a woman of her calibre to stoop to make any reply, I do this now for her. Tell Diderot that Mademoiselle de L'Espinasse is a creature of a sort most Parisians know only in the finest tragedies, that she has already suffered enough in this world (you know her story), without being tormented by a man who calls it philosophy to drag a person's good name through mud. Tell Diderot that I am Mademoiselle de L'Espinasse's most devoted servant, but that if my devotion might give any damage to her reputation then I would leave her at once and never set eyes on her again.

Diderot was my friend once. He is an able man, but he has sought celebrity where he should have sought truth. This saddens me deeply.

The Comte de Guibert to Claude Martigny.   *June 24 1772*

I have made an acquaintance which will, I am sure, be of great advantage to me. I mean Mademoiselle de L'Espinasse who, as you know, hosts the most illustrious salon in Paris. We were introduced a fortnight ago in the gardens of the Moulin Joli, and I was at once able to make a favourable impression upon her. She expressed considerable interest in my military achievements, and I told her of the work on tactics which I am preparing. So taken was she with this important scheme, that she invited me to attend her salon to speak about it.

Mademoiselle de L'Espinasse does not look forty, but is more like a very plain thirty year old. She has suffered from smallpox, which has left its mark, though even without its scars she could never have been pretty. She is tall, with a graceful figure, but does not dress well. In fact, she seems to take an absurd pride in being unwomanly, in being like the men she surrounds herself with (she has no female friends, and women find her an oddity). She has read everything, seen every play, opera and painting. Her life, it would seem, has been as lacking in passion as that of D'Alembert, who scuttles around her like a mother hen, shrieking and fussing over everything, laughing at her feeblest jokes. I almost feel pity for them. They were both orphans, of course; this is something which must have brought them together, along with their love of obscure knowledge, and their physical unattractiveness. They are well matched in fact, though the rumours which were quickly shared with me at the salon, that they were once lovers but that Mademoiselle de L'Espinasse rejected D'Alembert for a Spanish nobleman, seem incredible to me. The two of them in each other's arms, Mademoiselle de L'Espinasse and Monsieur d'Alembert, would be like the entwinement of two dry branches, gnarled and withered. And what must the Spaniard be like? The whispers (which were the liveliest feature of that salon of faded celebrities) gave me to understand that he is not yet thirty, a man no older than myself! He is apparently handsome, with a lively wit, but very unhealthy. I can therefore find only one common feature which might have drawn him to the sickly Mademoiselle de L'Espinasse.

How has this plain woman, a bastard child whom others of her sex find suspect, come to be one of the most influential figures in the intellectual and artistic life of Paris?

D'Alembert to J. C. de la Haye.   *July 19 1772*

Give yourself only to science. Do not expect to find happiness anywhere else. Fame is a mirage, it can evaporate as easily as a rainbow, it is a sparkling illusion in the eyes of those around you which, if you place too much trust in them, you will come to believe in as well. Believe only in yourself, and your work. Truth exists in mathematics, and nowhere else. You might give it all up for a woman (this is the reason, I now learn, why you have neglected your studies). What a waste this would be, what a crime! A dog in the street can chase a mate, but can it calculate the orbits of the planets? You are a scientist, not a dog. Chase mathematics, it will never disappoint you. Imagine what it would be like to spend ten years, or even twenty, on a most profound calculation. At the end of these years you believe you have found the solution, you feel triumphant. But then you discover that the object of your study does not exist, it has no meaning, it deceived you constantly, whenever it seemed to yield a little of its subtleties. Pursue the love of those around you, and this will be your fate. You abandon science for some girl, then what? Ten years from now she might turn round and tell you that she feels nothing for you, that her love was a delusion, and now that she can see clearly once more, she no longer needs you. If she is true now she will wait ten years for you, but will science wait? Will you still remember, ten years from now, how to comprehend those arcs, ellipses and parabolas which you currently manipulate with ease? They will not wait for you, while you play with women. Science will move on, others will steal the trophies which could be yours, you will be forgotten, you will grow old and then you will turn to dust and there will be nothing for you to leave behind.

In my life there has only really been one love, a love which by its nature could never be reciprocated but which has nevertheless sustained me through more than fifty years, and this is the love of mathematics. I have tried to direct my love elsewhere, but without success. Those objects to which I might have attempted to apply it proved unwilling, incapable of returning my affection except in a form which is little more than polite. I can see this now. But I have been privileged to know the kind of love which is unsoiled by being dependent on reward, which is pure and springs directly from the soul, from the seat of one's being. I have loved without regard to whether I might be loved in return. This has been the devotion I have given to mathematics, the balm of every ill. I am a scholar, I was born to the scholarly life, it was decreed at the very moment I was left, newly born, on the cold steps of a church many years ago. It was written on me then, that I should grow to be one who craves solitude, who fears the criticism and hostility of others, who seeks not to compete with the world but to escape from it, into a clearer realm where the insoluble problem of good and evil gives way to the light of reason and absolute logic. Only in mathematics have I found answers, nowhere else. Certainly not in the words and actions of the people among whom I pass each day.

When I was young I did all the work on which my reputation rests. Now I am old and my brain is too sluggish. I spend two weeks on a problem which once would have detained me for no more than an afternoon. For most of the time I do nothing at all that is of any worth. Do not waste your talents, and above all do not believe that the love or admiration of any person can ever be worth as much as your own research, and the beauty of knowing that what you have discovered is true and can never be disproved, can never be eradicated. Now is the time when you can find immortality. Like all young people you treat life as if it were eternal, you will soon learn otherwise. But you can do work now which will make your name last forever.

And you would give it all away for a woman!

Julie de L'Espinasse to the Comte de Crillon.   *August 2 1772*

Our new friend the Comte de Guibert is young, handsome, and fully aware of his talents. Like all great men he observes everything around him which may prove to be of use, and does not waste time looking within himself. There is something at once admirable and repellent about this. He is clearly a skilful tactician, in life as much as in war.

He is not without admirers, of course. Mademoiselle de Bouverie could not keep her eyes from him, and she is certainly a very attractive woman, though rather dull. I would not be surprised if they were to bond in some way (marriage is impossible, of course). Then there is Madame de Lancy, who would certainly be young enough for him and would probably be more useful.

I shall keep you informed of the progress of his career.

These days the appearance of a new face is like the explosion of a star in a forgotten constellation. Guibert has given everyone something to talk about. He is that sort of man; the kind who forces all whom he meets to form some opinion of him. Mine is that he is clever, ambitious and completely heartless. He practises those skills which befit great men; he is a fine soldier, he writes, he occupies a seat in the theatre where he listens carefully to the judgement of those who understand what they see. He is a man who will find success in whatever field he chooses to pursue, as long as it is one in which success means winning praise and admiration, nothing else.

He has set his sights on some goal (I am not sure what it may be, but it cannot be too hard to guess), and he will do whatever is necessary to achieve it. He will trample on anyone who comes in his way, he will flatter anyone who may be able to advance him. He is, in short, the perfect gentleman of our times, and we must all admire him.

Julie de L'Espinasse to the Comte de Mora. *October 28 1772*

So you are to leave Paris yet again! My heart is breaking. Though our meetings have always been brief, they have been like air to me. I fear I shall suffocate!

The times I have spent with you have been the only truly happy ones of my life. You have made me feel wanted and respected, you have brought such joy to me. How selfish of me to think only of what you bring to me, when I give so little in return, but your love is the kind which asks no fee. Without you Paris is dead again. Winter is here already, no bird sings. Do not stay long in Madrid. Write to me every day, tell me everything. The smallest detail, if it is observed by you, becomes great and wonderful. Be well again, and strong, and then come back to me.

At the salon of Mademoiselle de L'Espinasse I read part of my tragedy *The Constable of Bourbon*, which my hostess declared a work of genius. Her tears were quite genuine.

She is not a pretty woman, but her unusual manner is strangely charming. During my reading I often looked up to watch her reaction (I found myself drawn to her face, though there were many finer ones which might have caught my eye). I saw an expression which I found completely unfathomable, as if she were somewhere else. I could not tell if it was the face of a drowning woman which I saw, or of a nun filled with self-loathing, or else of a shrewd and scheming merchant, trying to find the best way to strike a deal. She is a mysterious woman, either completely frigid or uncontrollably passionate, though I cannot tell which. I should like to find out. It would amuse me.

Julie de L'Espinasse to the Comte de Crillon.   *November 11 1772*

Guibert visited me today, and for a little while I was able to escape from my sorrow. He is a striking and very gifted man, and speaks easily. But as soon as he had left I remembered the Comte de Mora, and my pain returned with even greater force.

You know how I feel about de Mora, I have often confided in you. But I am filled with a sense of hopelessness. For over six years I have lived in constant anguish! Now that he is away from Paris again I feel sure that I shall never have him, that I shall never find happiness.

While Guibert spoke of his projects, I could at least forget all this for a brief moment. He never sat down, refusing a seat but choosing instead to pace about the room like a general surveying his troops. Often he would go to the window and look out in a rather theatrical manner, as if caught by a stroke of inspiration. Then he would turn and pick up some new topic of conversation.

He is a vain man, but also very handsome. He has a confidence which is thrilling and quite terrifying. I mentioned

Mademoiselle de Maïs, whom I know has shown considerable interest in him, and he gave a shrug, saying he found
her charming, though misguided. He would not expand on
this, but he was clearly eager to make it seem that he had
shared a confidence with me. I then praised Madame Fro-
mont, another of his admirers, and again he seemed evasive.
What am I to make of this? Such idle games help at least to
distract me from the torment which my entire existence has
become.

The Comte de Guibert to Claude Martigny.   *January 25 1773*

My little campaign has been developing well, along precisely
those lines which I planned. Sometimes the sweetest victory
is won against the weakest opponent. Mademoiselle de
L'Espinasse is already devoted to me. She tells me to visit, and
almost as soon as I arrive is making the next appointment.
She writes letters to me in between, in which she speaks
warmly of our friendship.

I leave soon for Germany. She has made me promise to
write every day, though I told her she can hardly expect me
to keep such a vow. Am I to spend all my time writing, when
there will be so much else to do?

Now I must say farewell. I am expected at Madame
Montsauge's.

D'Alembert to Charles Mellier.   *April 8 1773*

I have been editing my works for a complete edition which
is now in preparation. To look again on the works of my
youth fills me with nostalgia. They were imperfect in many
ways, yet they have a freshness which touches me, across the
years. I was in love with my work then, it gave me such joy,
and my only regret was that I needed to waste so many hours
in unproductive sleep, when I could otherwise be thinking
and calculating. Now my work is that of a clerk, rearranging
papers, moving them from one place to another. My mind
has run out of ideas and energy. I am not far off sixty, and yet

my life seems to have vanished behind me in an instant. My collected works will fill many volumes, but will there be anything in them which people will find worth reading after I am gone?

My worries are added to by Mademoiselle de L'Espinasse's state of health. She eats little, her sleep is irregular. Although she usually retires early to bed, I believe that she often lies awake, gripped by pains in her chest, unable to breathe properly. She continues to entertain as much as ever, and also maintains her correspondence with her many friends, particularly the Comte de Mora and the Comte de Guibert, with both of whom she communicates every day. How she finds the strength to write so much I do not know. It cannot be good for her in her present condition. Yet even in ill health she maintains that enthusiasm for the trivial which can be so delightful when it is not exasperating.

Earlier today she came to me in great excitement to say that a cat had been found with a litter of kittens, hidden away in the coal cupboard. She told me this with such emotion, such concern in her voice that I felt moved by her compassion for the little creatures. It was a black and white cat, she told me (you see, she had visited the new family, given a saucer of milk to the mother). She wondered what would happen to the animals, and at the thought that they might die there were tears in her eyes. Everything which has life is, to her, equally important, equally to be valued. In fact, she sometimes shows less consideration for those around her than for the cats which treated her kindness with total indifference. Who is the more to be envied, I wonder: Mademoiselle de L'Espinasse, to whom all things are equal, or the cats, to whom all things are uncomprehended? Are my collected works worth more or less than a litter of cats? For the former, I might add, the wise Mademoiselle de L'Espinasse shows little interest.

The sun is shining now. I shall take a walk alone, as I am so fond of doing, and when I return I shall begin to read this beautiful volume of Lucretius which you have so kindly sent me.

Guibert made me swear not to tell anyone of his affairs, but if he cannot keep them secret he surely cannot expect anyone else to do the same. Besides, I am sure I was not the first to learn about his liaison with Mademoiselle de L'Espinasse.

As is well known, she has for several years been in love with the Comte de Mora, a sickly Spaniard whom many feel cannot have long to live. Now she has also thrown herself into the arms of Guibert. They fell in love before he left for Germany, and during his travels they exchanged countless letters. Guibert showed me several of hers, as well as copies of his elegant replies. Last week he returned to Paris, and on Wednesday night (he described it all to me very fully), he went to her apartment.

She had arranged things very carefully, anxious that his visit should go undiscovered. Monsieur d'Alembert, who watches over her like a governess, was out for the evening and would not return before midnight. Mademoiselle de L'Espinasse would go to bed at nine o'clock, the servants shortly afterwards. She told Guibert to wait beneath her window around half past nine until he saw a light go out in her room. This was the signal that he should go inside and upstairs to the door of her apartment, where she herself would let him in. Her greatest fear was that she would be discovered wandering about, in which case she would pretend to be sleepwalking and the servants would leave her alone, terrified by her condition and afraid to waken her. Once Guibert was inside, the good soldier would be able to follow her stealthily to her room.

The time came, and Guibert's carriage drew to a halt at the proper place. The signal was made, and our gallant friend went in. The porter was of no consequence, Guibert silently rewarded him and proceeded upstairs. Then he was let in, and the two of them went to Mademoiselle de L'Espinasse's chamber.

Shall I tell you what took place there? I could not possibly describe it as well as Guibert related it to me. Perhaps he will tell you the story himself.

Julie de L'Espinasse to the Comte de Guibert.   *February 17 1774*

Why do you want my love? What good will it do you? You already have the admiration of so many people, you let Madame de Montsauge think she is loved by you, you make both her and myself unhappy.

I loathe society. I wish only to find tranquillity in solitude, but you will not allow me this. If I could persuade Monsieur d'Alembert not to live with me I might begin to have peace, but while I feel this passion for you I know that I can find no rest. You torture me, even when you are kind to me.

I have learned, through many years, to live without happiness. But you have taught me pleasure, and I do not know if I can live without this. Tell Madame de Montsauge you cannot see her, make any excuse. Come to me now.

Francisco Castelar to Julie de L'Espinasse.
            Letter dated May 15 1774, delivered June 3 1774

My Lord the Conde de Mora died yesterday. He had been gravely ill since February, and when his death seemed certain he instructed me to bring him to Paris in order, he said, that he might resolve certain items of business. Our mission did not reach the Pyrenees before the Conde expired.

His end was a merciful one. After many days during which he had suffered great distress he finally lapsed into a deep sleep from which he never awakened, and which returned to his features that look of peace and youthful joy for which we shall all remember him. Though the Lord God may act strangely in taking from us so pure and noble a heart, and at such an early age, we must thank Him for allowing us to know a man who was just, kind and fair in all his dealings.

Before he lost consciousness he instructed me to notify you of his decease, to return to you all the letters which you have written to him, and which you find here enclosed, and to express to you his undying affection. It was, he told me, his intention on reaching Paris to ask for your hand in marriage. I need not tell you how much I am grieved, both by the passing of the beloved Conde, and by the duty which he entrusted to me to communicate his last message to you. We have lost the dearest man on earth.

Claude Martigny to the Comte de Crillon.   *June 12 1776*

I believe you knew Mademoiselle de L'Espinasse well, and knew also of her affair with the Comte de Guibert, a man the full extent of whose qualities are only now becoming apparent to me. I find it hard still to name as a friend one who can so easily break the hearts of two innocent people (D'Alembert and Mademoiselle de L'Espinasse) and regard it as some kind of triumph. His grief for his former lover is fulsome, the shallowness of his sentiment quite evident. Even now, so soon after Mademoiselle de L'Espinasse's death, he is speaking of his intention one day to publish her letters to him.

He had already abandoned her before the end, of course. After playing with her for a year and a half, he announced that it was time for him to marry, having chosen (as you are no doubt aware) the lovely Mademoiselle de Courcelles. It is hardly surprising that Mademoiselle de L'Espinasse, weakened by grief and opium, should so quickly have fallen ill with the fever which took her life last month.

Can it really be the case that D'Alembert knew nothing? Difficult to believe that the man who lived so close to her, who shared so much of his life with her, should have been ignorant of what was known to many. And yet it seems that this was the case, that it was only the letters which told him the truth, all the papers he discovered once she had closed her eyes and left him forever; the drafts she kept of all her correspondence, which he now had to file and catalogue, and all the replies from men who had stolen her from beneath his eyes. Can anyone imagine the agony with which his grief has been compounded? He wrote to Guibert (who showed me the letter, as if it were another of his trophies), a dignified letter, but one in which pain and despair were evident. D'Alembert had given his life to Mademoiselle de L'Espinasse, and those years of devotion were lost, as if they were no more than a dream which proves on waking to have been quite without substance. D'Alembert has seen his whole life evaporate, and can only look forward now to the final refuge of the grave.

He has left the Rue de Bellechasse, and gone to live in the Louvre, having taken the suite to which his position as Permanent Secretary of the Académie des Sciences entitles him. He is receiving no visitors.

I have written to him, expressing my sorrow, and in reply he asked me to give him whatever information I could concerning the life of the woman whom, he now realises, he never really knew. I have sent him various pieces of correspondence which can only increase his pain, but which the sincerity of his request prevents me from withholding. You may wish to do likewise, and contact anyone else who may be able to assist Monsieur d'Alembert. He spent years working on the *Encyclopédie;* now this last work of his is the most painful research of all.

Mademoiselle de L'Espinasse's salon was the finest in Paris, her passing is like the fall of an empire. I hear that when word of her death reached her estranged aunt Madame du Deffand (who is now of course in her eighties), the blind old woman said: "Once this news would have grieved me. Now it means nothing at all."

VIII

Justine stood up and went back to the drawing room. The visitor who had been waiting there had gone, she had not heard him depart. He had left behind the manuscript he had brought for D'Alembert, which was called *The Cosmography.*

She picked it up and took it with her back to the study. Henri would return soon, surely. His errands could not detain him much longer.

In the study she found D'Alembert still lying in exactly the same position. He had not moved at all while she had been reading. Was he all right? From his open mouth, though she listened closely, there was no longer any whistling of his breath. She shook his shoulder, and then shook it again, harder, until she knew at last that he was dead. He looked as if he had gone into the most peaceful kind of sleep.

She pulled his head back, trying to make him sit upright in the chair. As she lifted him a hoarse wheezing came from deep within his chest which made her let out a scream, but she realised that it was no more than his last trapped breath. How long had he held it there? At what moment while Justine was beside him did his soul find peace at last? Though upright in his chair now, his head was still turned to the side, long grey hair sticking to his cheek. She wiped his face, made him sit as he had done in life only hours before, when she had watched him write. She knew him now, after all that she had read. He was more alive to her than during all the six years she had served him. She only wished she had known him sooner.

She was unsure what to do with the document which the strange visitor had left. As for D'Alembert's manuscript, she realised now that he had written it for no one other than himself, and although she had sinned by reading it, what she had learned made her respect her master enough not to wish the sin to be repeated on countless other occasions. She must burn it. And she would burn the letters too, she would take everything out into the yard and watch the charred fragments rise and float into oblivion, since she knew that this was what the master would wish; that his pain had been shared now, with her, and needed no further balm.

She would gather everything up in a moment. But first she would read the final part of D'Alembert's manuscript; the page on which his face had lain.

IX

Do I wake now, or sleep? I saw my life, or at least I think it was my life, though how can I still be sure that it really was my own, and not someone else's? My life has been a treatise written by an ancient hand, a series of propositions following from first principles, each event inevitable and ordained by logic. It was written even before I lay crying on some cold steps, a baby wrapped in a bundle of rags, as if I had been dropped from heaven. If those equations which mapped my course had not been discovered by me, then some other soul would have followed the chain of logic which has led me to my eventual destination.

It seems the light is fading. How long have I been sitting here? I find myself forgetting so much now. Gradually my past is dissolving behind me, like the waves which follow a boat. I look back and I see that the lost years are spreading out, diffusing and dispersing in the wake of my long course through the world. Julie, Diderot, Madame du Deffand, they are like stars flying apart, galaxies and vast clouds of dark matter hurtling through cold empty space. Yes, I am returning now to that dark coldness which first gave me life. I raise my face and look upwards, all is dark, and I see a great figure above me. Could it be the face of the one who found me, as I lay in a bundle of rags? I see the dark and endless universe, the brightness of tiny stars, and I feel at last the warmth of a hand, reaching down towards me. I shall not be left here to be forgotten forever. There is some greater love which floats down onto me out of the silent darkness like a flake of snow, and touches my closing eyelids.

All around me there is bright sunlight. I am a child again, and I am with my friend Bernard. He is taller than me, good looking. Everyone likes him, but this summer he has chosen me as his favourite, and I love him for it. We are playing marbles in the sand, the sun is high above us, and the sand is warm to the touch. As the marbles hit one another they throw up little clouds of dust. Bernard says: "What will you do when you grow up, D'Alembert?" I look down at the glass marbles in the sand and I see great questions, deep problems. I see a life of glory and achievement, many lives coming together, flying apart again, in endless motion.

"When I grow up I'm going to be an astronomer," I tell him, "and find out what makes the stars move. What about you, Bernard?"

"I don't ever want to grow up," he says. "I want to go on playing marbles with you, like this, for ever and ever."

And so we carry on playing, in the endless heat of the sun.

THE *COSMOGRAPHY* OF
MAGNUS FERGUSON

INTRODUCTION

Magnus Ferguson was born in Strathaird in 1712, the son of a draper. A gifted child, he taught himself from books, and went to Edinburgh in 1730 to seek his fortune. There he fell in with the so-called "Kilmartin Club", a group of Catholic artists, intellectuals and assorted hangers-on who had as their figurehead the flamboyant and ill-fated Earl of Blantyre. It was this powerful patron who enabled Ferguson to carry out his philosophical researches. In addition, Ferguson was able to participate in the scenes of disordered revelry for which the "Club" became notorious.

The only personal account we have concerning Ferguson comes from a fellow Club member, Athanasius Scobie, whose *Memoirs of an Illustrious Scoundrel* were privately published in Italy in 1783. That original work (a limited edition circulated amongst a small number of friends and admirers of the poet) appears to have been lost; all that survives is an Italian translation of 1803, in which it is clear that even those portions which genuinely are by Scobie are in many cases the fanciful inventions of an ageing syphilitic romanticising about the long-lost days of his youth. Nevertheless Scobie was a cultured and intelligent man, who clearly had a good understanding of Ferguson's ideas, and his account of the philosopher betrays a warmth which would seem to indicate something more genuine than senile confabulation, or the interpolations of an imaginative translator. The following extract (which is a retranslation of the Italian text) serves as the only source we have of Ferguson's philosophy, as it was set out by him in his lost essay "*A Natural History of the Human Soul*", and provides a fitting introduction to the *Cosmography*, his only surviving work.

After drinking and talking late into the night we poured out onto the street, a whole gang of us light-headed and merry. Semple spoke of poetry, Garvie of women, the rest of us talked all at once and listened to none. Someone was holding my arm, helping me to walk a straight path.

The route to Joe Hendry's was a long one, our steps were uneven, and our drunken party soon became strung out like beads of stray spittle on a sailor's beard. Someone was keeping hold of me, Ferguson and Arnott were a good way ahead, and as we rounded a corner to follow them I saw dimly by the moonlight that they had become engaged in conversation with a group of young men, five or six of them perhaps, gathered in a semicircle, and already one of them was pulling his shoulders back and straightening up for a quarrel. It seemed that some disagreement had arisen between the two parties, we went more quickly so as to join our friends, and as we came near, one of the strangers drew a blade or cudgel, my companion ran to safety and Ferguson and Arnott turned to escape, but upon those two the other members of the gang quickly fell. My friends collapsed to the ground beneath the heavy on-slaught, a ruthless volley of kicks and punches, and as I moved forward to assist them I saw to my side another of the ruffians, holding something in his hand which he raised in readiness to strike.

What I felt was a great blow to the side of my head, which sent me falling to the ground beside the others. It may have been a knife which my assailant used, or else perhaps a broken bottle or some other weapon. I was aware of blood everywhere; and its taste in my mouth, a strangely metallic flavour, told me that it must be my own. It was on my arms, my clothes, on the ground where I lay. If the gang were still kicking me, then I noticed none of it. My mouth was so full of fluid that I feared I might choke. I tried to sit up, raising myself by one arm from the cobbles and tilting my head so as to empty my mouth, and as I did so I was aware of the right side of my face falling away, like a slice of meat from a roast joint. The blow had pierced my cheek in a horizontal line several inches long, leaving the flesh of my jaw to hang freely.

The blood was everywhere, all over the ground and my clothes. My shirt felt drenched with it, as if I had emerged from a river, and my mind was swirling, clear and yet somehow detached from my experience, as though this river of blood still held me, and I were drowning in it.

At some point our attackers ran off, horrified perhaps by the sight of their own work. I was sitting up, holding my cheek in place with my hand, and Ferguson was at my side, bleeding profusely himself, but tearing strips from his own shirt with which to try and bind my wound. Arnott had bravely got up to run in pursuit of the gang, hoping to rejoin the rest of our companions so as to retaliate in strength. Ferguson meanwhile tied my face up with the torn scraps of his clothing. I remember the warmth of his hands, and the gentleness with which he tended to my wounds, quite ignoring his own injuries.

I was able to stand now. Ferguson supported me, and we made our way to Joe Hendry's. As we walked together in silence, I shuddered at the recollection of what had happened, the sudden outburst of violence which had occurred for no reason. While I lay bleeding I had felt strangely calm, but now fear was beginning to overpower me. Ferguson explained later that a similar experience had happened to him. As he lay curled on the ground, the kicks and blows had gradually come to feel lighter, as if he were being struck not by boots and fists, but by pillows or heavy sacks whose force was dull and painless.

"And the strangest thing," he later told me, "was that I suddenly felt I was no longer myself. I don't know if it was as if I was another person, or else no-one at all. But my sense of my own identity, my own existence, completely disappeared for a moment."

I had experienced something similar, though not perhaps so extreme. In any event, the brutal episode that night formed a bond between us which would never be broken. We reached Joe Hendry's, and in the light there the extent of my injuries was so plain that a woman fainted at the sight and had to be carried out. Ferguson was badly bruised but otherwise relatively uninjured, and he sat silently in a corner holding a poultice to his gashed forehead while a surgeon was called for, who stitched up my cheek with catgut, and of all the ordeals which I endured that evening, the surgeon's work on me was the most hellish. Even the half-pint of whisky they gave me could not mask the pain, though I had already been drinking all evening. I cursed and swore between clenched teeth each time the surgeon's needle pierced my flesh, and I felt the catgut being dragged through, as large and coarse to my senses as if it were a length of rope. Ferguson sat silently in the corner throughout.

Some months later, we had occasion to discuss the incident, and this was when he told me of his singular impression concerning his own identity; the fleeting sensation while the blows landed on his body that he was not himself. I had seen little of Ferguson in the intervening period, but I was to learn that he had been at work on his great philosophical essay entitled *A Natural History of the Human Soul*. He told me that the beating had been a kind of revelation to him, it had made him aware that one's soul is in reality a kind of sense, like that of touch or taste, and it was a sense which could become impaired or defective, or perhaps could be deceived. He had set out to imagine what it would be like for an individual to be "blind" to his own identity, just as a man might be blind to light. In other words, Ferguson tried to imagine a person who was rational and yet unaware of his own existence, like a sightless man unable to see his own reflection. This had caused him to invent a character named William McDade, and in his essay (part of which I had the opportunity to read), Ferguson imagines that he visits this unfortunate McDade and has a lengthy discussion with him. For example, he asks McDade how he feels, and McDade replies that the notion of feeling has no meaning for him, since it presupposes a subject who experiences that feeling. For McDade, a statement can only be meaningful if it is objectively verifiable. Asked how it can be possible for him to reply so lucidly to Ferguson's questioning, when McDade claims not to be aware of his own existence (at one point even seeking to disprove it), McDade proposes the analogy of a mechanical automaton which has the power of speech, and can appear to use language meaningfully, and yet must be assumed to be without consciousness.

Ferguson concludes that it is impossible to convince McDade that he really exists, and that it is equally impossible to imagine what it would be like to be in McDade's position, since McDade cannot truly be said to have any experience of his illness, or indeed of anything at all. He cannot know what it feels like to be himself.

This shadowy figure, the subject of a memorable literary fantasy filled with profound philosophical insight, had occurred to Ferguson in the aftermath of that terrible and unprovoked attack we had sustained. I had done my best to forget the incident; Ferguson, on the other hand, saw it as one of the most significant events of his life. McDade has remained in my memory just as much as Ferguson. In a sense, McDade is the person whom Ferguson became during that moment of torture when his own existence seemed open to doubt. And yet, while nature decrees that those phantoms which may haunt the agony of souls near death should be swept away as soon as life returns triumphant, Ferguson had endeavoured to capture the phantom, to prevent its return to the world of the unliving. Ferguson wished to preserve it, to study its manners, habits and customs. This McDade was the manifestation of a dying soul, a spirit set free from the chains of personal identity. McDade embodied that great river into which all souls must one day flow, a river which Ferguson, after that moment of revelation in an Edinburgh street, could no longer fear. McDade is therefore not to be pitied, even though Ferguson's story of him presents a man disabled by a crucial mental impairment. Rather, we should see McDade as the most liberated of all men.

This episode in Ferguson's essay is the most memorable, but in addition he covered a great many other questions besides, few of which made any sense to me. I do however recall the Paradox of the Lottery, which Ferguson explained to me in some detail.

Imagine then that a thousand people are each allocated a numbered ticket (no two players being given the same number), and a winner is drawn by lot. Clearly, for each person there is a one in a thousand chance of success. Ferguson then proposed a second game, in which three curious dice are rolled, each of which has ten equal faces (rather than the usual six) numbered 0 to 9; the player winning if he rolls a treble zero. Once again, a simple computation shows the probability of success to be one in a thousand; however, there is a crucial difference between the two games. It is possible that the second game will not produce a winner, even after more than a thousand rolls of the dice. The lottery, on the other hand, must certainly bring success to one lucky player, every time it is run. It would seem then that the lottery might somehow be a more profitable game to play, even though one is in theory no more likely to win at it than at the dice game.

In order to resolve this apparent paradox, Ferguson proposed the following interpretation of the dice game. Whenever the three dice are rolled, a thousand different worlds come into being, in each of which a different score has been thrown. The man who rolls three ones, for example, is no more than a single point in a thousandfold universe, each one of which contains another possible ramification of his fate. It is then certain that the player will win in one of these many worlds; all that remains open to doubt is whether the winning world will coincide with the one in which the player believes himself to exist.

Ferguson concluded, in other words, that at every instant in time, all the various outcomes which can arise from any given situation produce an ever-branching hierarchy of possible universes. In fact, he even went so far as to suggest that these many worlds were eternal, and had existed for all time, so that a person's life merely consists of the gradual tracing out of a single path amongst their infinite bifurcations. When for example those ruffians set about us in the street, there was a world (or rather many worlds) in which Ferguson died, and many more in which his survival took various forms (in some he emerged a cripple, in others his wounds were negligible). During that moment of indecision, when Ferguson's body was being battered and pounded, he had for a moment seen before him the infinite vista of diverging paths, some leading to death, others to life. He, Ferguson, was destined to follow one of those paths; perhaps his course was decreed from the very moment of primordial creation. But there were other Fergusons, other souls who must proceed along different avenues. His soul was not one but many, branching and splitting with every passing moment. It was only in that moment of greatest crisis, when so many possible paths seemed to lead to annihilation, that their differing directions had made some hazy impression on his senses. He was, in that moment, an infinity of souls, and hence also none.

Ferguson considered putting in his essay a dedication to the celebrated David Hume. Hume however never saw the work, and would hardly have been expected to approve of it if he had. From an empiricist's point of view, Ferguson's universe of possible worlds is an absurdity, its infinite branches being by definition unobservable (except during moments of mystical vision), and forever beyond the possibility of proof or refutation. Their existence was, as Ferguson put it, "an article of faith, kept aloft by the conviction that Nature must in all its ways be logical and complete." In other words, Ferguson believed that the truth of the world could be discovered by logical analysis. In fact, he even went so far as to assert that all forms of observation are inherently inaccurate and misleading, and that experimental science could only cause confusion.

I do not know what became of Ferguson. The defeat of 1745 shattered our brotherhood. The Earl of Blantyre fled to France, where he died of cholera. It is possible that Ferguson accompanied him, or else that he shared the fate of Arnott and Dalwhinnie, who were hanged. Or else he disappeared, his past conveniently erased.

All of these eventualities must certainly have occurred in some world, if not in our own.

The precise date of composition of the *Cosmography* is unknown, its authenticity (and even Ferguson's very existence) having been questioned on a number of occasions. No original manuscript survives; the earliest handwritten copies are fragmentary and in many cases contradictory. One portion (the so-called Paris Text) is known to have been in the possession of Jean le Rond d'Alembert, some of the sheets having been used by his servants to wrap the effects of the mathematician after his death in 1783 (the remainder were presumably destroyed). It is not known how D'Alembert came to possess the manuscript, nor what he made of it. Its existence might lend some support to Scobie's suggestion that Ferguson could have ended his days in France, though it is just as probable that one of Ferguson's admirers was responsible for transmitting the work to that country.

Several other secondary manuscripts exist, and stylistic variations suggest many rewritings and alterations by different hands over the years. The successive reworkings of incomplete sources means that Ferguson's single extant work is in fact many, the notional authorship of this assortment of Cosmographies suggesting a plurality wholly in keeping with Ferguson's supposed philosophy. The version given here is itself a composite of several of these sources, with some insertions made for the sake of continuity. Given the history of the work, this further contribution to its changing form will, I hope, be judged leniently.

The "Prologue" given in Clark's edition is almost certainly spurious, but is included here for completeness:

To His Grace, the Duke of B——,
  Sir,
You are too kind in your enquiries after me, and in your concern over my absence. I have been on a long journey, much farther than anything I had intended, and have seen many things which I hope you will allow me the indulgence of relating to you.

Bound for Denmark, where as you know I hoped to present my philosophical discoveries to the King, our ship was caught up in a great storm. The sea and sky grew black and roared most terribly, and we all felt sure that we should be killed. A monstrous wind struck the deck where I stood clinging to a wooden rail. A piece of the rail came away in my hand as I was carried into the air. My senses failed me, I fell into a daze, yet still I was borne aloft by the hurricane, lifted high into the air, beyond the clouds, and into darkest space.

When I awoke I found myself lying on the surface of the Moon. I was slightly bruised from my landing, but otherwise unhurt, and still held the broken fragment of wooden rail in my hand. I got up and began to look around. Let me tell you, Sir, that at close quarters the Moon is in fact highly hospitable, its many trees having silvery leaves which give the appearance of barren rock to observers on the Earth. The famous lunar seas contain a fluid which, although not water, is nevertheless drinkable and indeed quite palatable. After walking for some time I met a group of Moon people, whom I found to be of pleasant appearance, and most friendly. They took me to their tent and gave me a strange cheese to eat, and after I had rested they showed me some of the sights and features of their world. They sail upon the lunar seas in boats not unlike our own, but in addition they have also devised vessels which travel through space, pushed swiftly by the strong breeze which, I learned, pervades every region of the Universe. After spending some days in their company, the Moon people gave me one such vessel in order that I might use it to return to my own world. I soon found, however, that the craft was not easy to steer, and in addition a combination of poor navigation and natural curiosity led me to visit each of the other planets before eventually returning to Earth. I humbly offer to you now my account of the wonders I discovered.

THE COSMOGRAPHY

This is a planet of dreams; though whether they are my own or those of some other, I cannot yet decide. I know only that everything I see here, the people with whom I come in contact, are all unreal.

To know unreality, to experience it vividly, can seem a strange phenomenon, though it is one with which we are familiar every day. When I read a book and see characters appear, I know these to be illusions, but the sensation is not a disconcerting one. Sometimes too, in our sleep, we may suddenly become aware that what we are seeing is no more than the product of our dreaming mind. This can seem like a moment of great insight, or comfort, or perhaps even sadness.

It is with such sensations that the visitor to this place is constantly filled. I see an elegant room, gilded furniture, fine porcelain upon a table. I know all of it to be unreal. The shapes around me have the appearance of solidity, they have weight, texture, permanence (I close my eyes, reopen them. Everything is still there, as it was). These objects display the superficial gloss of reality, yet do nothing to convince me of their existence. In the world from which I come, the reality of objects is taken for granted; here, on the other hand, the converse is true, it is their subjectivity which is immediately clear; to believe in their validity is something requiring great mental effort. Whatever is apparent (even transparent) in my own world, here is opaque; what seems obvious here, would be a matter there for philosophical debate.

I pick up a cup of blue and white porcelain, which appears to have been made in China. I drop it to the floor (marble), where it smashes, making a sound. The authenticity of these events, the vividness of the sensations they evoke, are quite unimpeachable, even though they are an artifact of my intellect. I cannot remember having seen precisely these objects, in this combination, in the world from which I come, yet I feel that I must have done so; that what I appear to experience is a synthesis of recollections. It impresses me, however, that my memory can have been so accurate, so flawlessly detailed. Do I really carry in my mind a picture of a china cup as perfect as this? I study the broken fragments, every carefully painted brushstroke of blue cobalt: a landscape, an oriental bridge and a pagoda, a comical figure bent under the bundle of sticks he carries. Was all of this contained within my memory, though I was not even aware of it? Or could I possibly have imagined it in such detail?

I decide to explore further. I leave the room in which I have found myself, and soon discover a library, where I open the glass door of one of the cases and pull out a volume at random. It is a minor Roman author (Aelian; his *Nature of Animals*), and not a book which I have ever read or heard of. Its text seems, as I leaf through the book, to have existed before I look at it. This fact appears paradoxical, and puzzles me. I read, and try to believe in Aelian's existence; I try to imagine that the words are his, the words of a real man (I cannot remember ever having heard of the author's name. How could I have spontaneously invented him and his work so quickly?). And yet I find the task an impossible one. The book is another dream. I put it back in its place, and close the door of the bookcase.

A small key would be needed in order to lock the door. It occurs to me to go in search of it. The drawers of a large bureau contain some letters (which intellectual curiosity encourages me to read, though they contain nothing worth reporting); also a pair of spectacles, which do not improve my own eyesight and are clearly those of someone else. I decide to continue my exploration of the grand house.

Upstairs, the door to one of the rooms is locked. When I knock on it, an elderly gentleman opens the door and invites me inside to join him. He has pulled his leather chair close to the warmth of the fire; I do likewise with a second chair, and we sit in silence together, watching the flickering of the flames. At length I decide to speak.

"Tell me, sir; how can you prove to me that you exist? You appear real enough to me, and yet I know that you cannot be."

The gentleman smiled, and said: "Can you be sure that the impression you speak of, that I am not real, is not itself another illusion?"

I conceded this point. Perhaps, I suggested, it would be as well to carry on as if the world were real after all.

"That," said the gentleman, "would be a grave error, and would surely lead you into philosophical difficulties."

I asked him to expand on this, but he seemed more interested in the warmth of the fire, whose glow was lighting up his face.

I said, "Do those spectacles in a drawer downstairs belong to you?"

He told me he knew of no such spectacles.

"I can bring them here to show you if you like."

He replied that this was not necessary; that the spectacles existed in my own subjective experience, but not necessarily in his. In order to refute him, I hurried back downstairs to the library, where I located them, put them in my pocket, and went quickly back. I then brought out the spectacles to show him. He displayed no interest, but only continued to maintain that the spectacles belonged to my subjective experience and not to his. I asked him to hold them, which he did, and I asked him if he now could feel their weight.

"My apparent experience of their weight belongs to your reality, and not to mine," he said.

All of this perplexed me deeply. I sat down once again in the leather armchair, and remained for some time in silence. Then after a while I said to my companion: "I should like to know about your subjective experience."

"That is not something which it is possible for you to know. All I can do is tell you the story of my experience, so that it may become a part of your own."

"Do you live here, on this planet?"

"Of course I do. This planet is the Earth, and everyone lives here. This castle is my own property, surrounded by five thousand acres of some of the richest land in Scotland. I am a man of wealth and power."

"And yet you exist only in my own mind."

"That is indeed the case. Though you will at least allow me to add that you also exist only in mine."

I got up, and prepared to leave. "This is a planet of paradoxes," I said. "None of this exists, and yet its apparent permanence is infallible. I left your spectacles in a drawer, I went back to find them, and they were still there. How can this be the case if they are not real?"

"Your philosophy will only lead you into confusion, my dear friend. What does your intuition tell you?"

"That you and everything else here is a fiction, conjured up by my own brain."

"Then that is the voice to which you should give heed."

I left the room. He told me that I was in Scotland; I knew that this could not be the case. And yet he also told me that the world around me was without substance, and on this I was forced to agree. I went downstairs, then out of the castle, passing through its fine entrance into the sunlight (the light of a sun which, I knew, had no reality). I walked along invented paths, across well-cut lawns which lived only in my memory, or in my dreams, and then I ventured into the imagined cool of a forest, where I saw a woman sitting on a bank near a stream. As I approached she gave a start, turned to look at me, and I saw that although she was not young, her face was kind and handsome. I told her not to be afraid of me, that I was lost and wished to know the way to the nearest town. She said she would take me there, and we walked together until we reached a small village which seemed familiar, though I could not name it. Certain buildings evoked a feeling of recognition, but were altered or relocated in such a way as to make them incapable of precise identification. It was clear to me that these subtle deformations were the result of imperfect memory; the illusion was vivid, but could not completely deceive me. I knew the village to be as false as the woman who escorted me there; products of my mind alone.

I was emboldened by the thought that in this place there was no truth, no reality. If I were to turn round and strike dead any person who passed me by, I would commit no crime, since my victim would be no more than a dream. In a similar way, I felt no embarrassment in asking my guide if I might stay with her, since I had nowhere else to go. She took me to her house, and told me that she had lived alone since the death some years earlier of her husband, who had fallen victim to typhoid during an outbreak of the disease.

The woman's name was Margaret, and her home was a simple one, pieced together from fragments of my memory. It reminded me in fact of the house in which I was born and spent the first few years of my life. Gazing at the timbers of the ceiling, and a long crack which ran across the white plastered surface between those timbers, I felt such a surge of nostalgia that it became easy for a moment to believe that I really had returned to my place of origin, that I was not lost among the stars, that the fissure in the white plaster, so vivid to my eyes, was not merely a filament of inter-stellar matter, spun out by imagination into another part of this great dream. A dream which might belong to my own mind, or else to the one whose sleep had given me existence.

We ate together − food whose texture and rich flavour were most convincing. And then as night drew on the time came to retire to bed, and Margaret showed no objection when I went with her to her chamber and then lay down beside her. She noticed a scar on my forehead, and I explained how I had acquired it some years earlier, when I was attacked by ruffians in a street in Edinburgh.

"Where is that place?" she asked. "I have never heard of it."

"Are we not in Scotland?" I said. I was not sure whether I had dreamed her to be ignorant, or else had conjured up a world in which the city no longer existed. She merely laughed, as if at my naivety, and drew her fingers across my brow as she lay back beside me. Through her white shift, her breasts looked warm and soft to the touch. I reached out to her, then buried my face in her body and moved myself on top of her, feeling the smooth cloth of her gown slide beneath my grip as I lifted it from her body. Her skin existed in my senses that night with a permanence which would out-live anything else I was to discover in this world.

Her husband, she told me after our love-making, had been a philosopher named Magnus Ferguson. These words did not surprise me, nor did I seek (as one who dreamt them in ordinary sleep might feel compelled) to try and see in them some weight or symbolic value. She had been married to someone who bore my own name, who seemed in many details quite like myself, in others wholly different (my own features evoked no recognition from her). I did not feel it necessary to pursue this fact. The other Ferguson was dead of typhoid, and I had come to replace him for a single night. She said that her husband had never pleased her so fully as I had just done, and this gave me quiet satisfaction.

Was that other Ferguson really myself? Or was it he, the one who died, who was the real Ferguson, and I merely an impostor? I refused to be troubled by such thoughts. The warmth of Margaret's body, though I never ceased to believe it to be an illusion, was enough to make me put aside these questions.

Next morning, I asked to know more about her husband. Margaret told me that he had been employed by the Duke of B——, who lived in the fine castle not far from the village. This, I surmised, must be the gentleman with whom I had my earlier interview. Ferguson had written a book with which to entertain his employer, describing Ferguson's sup-posed voyages to the planets. She told me that a copy of the manuscript remained in her possession, and when I asked to see it she brought it from the chest where it was preserved. On the cover I saw the title: *The Cosmography of Magnus Ferguson*. Opening it, I immediately recognised the first chapter to be in my own handwriting:

Mercury

When I arrived on this planet I began to walk, and as I looked behind me, I saw that each part of me was still there which had occupied my immediate past. Time here is not a single stream of events, but an eternally present ramification of possibilities.

If you raise your arm, you see a trail of images which remain even when your limb has reached its finishing point. The arm, or something of it, somehow remains simultaneously in each of its intermediate positions. One's vision here is blurred by the constant interference of one's past and alternative possible present.

On a dusty track (for so I took it to be) I encountered a fork, one path leading to the left, the other to the right. After some indecision I took the left, but saw another self choose the right. I watched my own figure walk off and disappear along that road, leaving in its wake the usual hazy trail of former steps, vacated positions. It too, this other self, would later split, whenever another choice became necessary, just as I myself continued to see other copies of my own figure leave and walk away at every junction, point of hesitation or alteration to my route.

I am one among many here. If I remain long enough, the entire planet will become populated through my own indecision, through the manifestation of choices not taken. It is not only outside my body that such events take place. I choose to remember my home, I also choose not to think of certain things, and yet I begin to see them, parallel thoughts which I am unable to resist, as new images of my own mind create themselves. All that I had ever avoided, all that I had feared in myself or never dared to put into practice, I see it all multiplying before my sight, a planet overrun with the monsters of uncontrolled imagination. I feel my brain becoming populated with a million lost alternatives.

And yet, throughout the terror of this ordeal, I remain myself, or what I think of as myself: a single dusty path across a great uncertain plain. Am I one man or many? Or else, am I a millionth part of some other, greater man, an infinitesimal fraction of that space of possibilities of which this world consists? Even when I leave, all the others will remain; those selves who decide to stay here forever, watching the endless unravelling of their fate.

This passage evoked a distant memory. The possibility that I really had invented those words (before imagining them to be on a page before me) could not altogether be discounted. The Ferguson who wrote the text and the Ferguson who read it were different creatures, yet also in some sense one. These thoughts perplexed but did not trouble me; the multiple personalities of one's own dream-world should not be any cause for worry. The next chapter which I turned to, however, was harder to fathom.

Venus

Floating palaces adorn this world, borne on soft winds which never cease, but caress the skin with gentle warmth. This planet is governed by the endless motion of fluids; turbulence induces anxiety, eddies promote peace and stability. Thoughts flow with the tides and currents which the orbits of the planets bring about. To think here, or to feel, is to experience a certain kind of motion.

In his drifting palace, a Duke is troubled by the uneasy waves on which his thoughts are carried. A memory floats by, swept helplessly past him, beyond his grasp. He rises from the throne, tries to reach out, but already it is gone. Another thought bobs past, half submerged in the current. To try and scoop it up is futile; if the stream chooses to bring it within his reach then this is what will happen. Otherwise it will disappear, like everything else. The anxious Duke watches his worries pour out of him, he sees his fears before him, blurring his vision, before they too are swept away.

Now another idea is reaching him, another memory is teasing him. Is it her again, or else some other seeking vengeance? From where he sits, the future is an uncertain threat, a distant agitation. Ripples are reaching him, messages from his courtiers lapping against him, perturbing his rest. Even when he sleeps they continue, and again there are those imperfect memories, in which his dreams become submerged: lost days, and friends who now wish to betray him.

New thoughts appear on the horizon, new impressions, which will arrive and be experienced, just as they have been known already by those other inhabitants, those other Dukes far across the globe, whose past will become his own present. Yet he will see it only as it arrives, that great dark tidal wave which will sweep him from his throne, flailing helplessly, but carried under, crushed and drowned, a memory himself now waiting to be carried lifeless into the mind of some other, further downstream, who will also then know the agony of uncertainty, the fear of imminent catastrophe. A wave which will continue, until the storm is dissipated in the collapse of a thousand thrones.

The obscurity of this passage reassured me that it could not have been composed by myself (though it seemed once again to have come from my own hand). I imagined, though, that if Ferguson (the other Ferguson) had addressed these words to his master the Duke of B——, then there might be some hidden meaning in them. A possibility suggested itself to me, a random guess. I asked Margaret, "Was the Duke your lover?"

She lowered her eyes, then said that the old man had forced himself upon her, and that to resist him would have threatened the welfare of her husband. "It was in order to escape from the shame he felt on discovering what had happened that my husband began writing. He retreated into fantasy." Margaret looked up again, then reached for my arm. I felt the same gentle grip, the same soft caress by which the night had been made to slip away like sand through a glass. "Do you think me wicked?" she asked. "I betrayed my husband while he was alive, and I have betrayed him again with you now that he is dead."

Since she did not exist, the question of morality did not arise, and so I chose not to discuss it. "Do you have any more of Ferguson's papers or belongings?"

She told me that following his death most of his effects had remained in the Duke's castle. Not wishing to have any more contact with her former lover, Margaret had been unable to recover them. I decided to return there immediately to find whatever I could.

As I stood up to leave she asked, "Will I ever see you again?"

"I am sure that there will be many more Magnus Fergusons," I replied.

Arriving at the castle, I found the entrance to the house to be open, as it had been when I left the previous day, and I went in freely without encountering any person. Before going upstairs, I decided to visit the library once more.

In a drawer, I saw again the spectacles (had the elderly Duke replaced them himself?) and the pile of imaginary letters, their content miraculously unchanged since the previous day. I went to one of the bookcases, and opened its glass door. A row of scientific books met my eye: Tribullus' *Mineralogy*, the *Menagerie* of Petrus Augustus, Dawson's *Motion of Vapours* . . . I knew each of these works very well. Might the bookcase now be presenting me with familiar images, having run out of further invention? So as to pursue the test more fully, I drew out Thomas Hughes' *Mechanics* and opened it at the first page. In the margin I saw a pencilled inscription in my own handwriting, one which moreover I could remember making. I reasoned furthermore that if my experience was simply the result of memory or imagination, then this discovery was the least remarkable of all the things I had so far encountered.

Each of the books in the case, I soon realised, had come from my own collection. I drew out a great many and leafed through them, finding within their pages my own comments and amplifications. One of the volumes fell open at a place marked by the insertion of an envelope. Putting the makeshift bookmark in my pocket, I began to read the passage which I found:

Montanus speaks of time as an endlessly flowing river in which we stand, while Philip of Norfolk has asserted that we should rather think of time as a stationary channel of water on which we are constrained by God to sail until our final day, our motion being governed in speed and direction by a Divine breeze. Pierre Tourraine, on the other hand, imagines the world to be illustrated on a great narrow tapestry, many leagues in length, which may be read in either direction.

But can we be sure, Pierre goes on to ask, that the universe may be portrayed on a single tapestry, rather than many? Might one's own life be no more than a single version of a story woven on an infinite number of perpetually unwinding sheets? And could one then travel sideways in time, as one moves between adjacent strips?

The book was Ashford's *Form and Transformation*. I closed it and then went upstairs, where I found the elderly gentleman I had met the previous day still in his chair by the fire.

"Who are you?" I said to him. "And where are the rest of my belongings?"

He looked up at me and smiled. "I am the Duke of B——, and those things of which you speak have no objective reality. Do not concern yourself with them."

"Then what of the man who worked here, whose books you still possess?"

"Those books are my own."

"Is the handwriting in their margins also yours?"

He looked at me with eyes moistened by infinite pity. "There is no handwriting in my books. My library exists only in my subjective experience, its contents can never be available to you."

I was angered by his stubbornness, but knew that there would be no point in showing him objects whose existence he would flatly deny. "What sort of creature are you?" I cried.

"I am a man of wealth and power, though these things mean nothing to me. I retired here in order to escape a world which I found to be hollow and worthless. For a while I employed a man named Magnus Ferguson who was to assemble for me a library with which I might complete the studies from which I had been distracted by the folly of youthful ambition. This task was still hardly begun when Ferguson died."

"But I am Magnus Ferguson," I said, "and you exist only in my mind. Of both these facts I am wholly sure."

He turned his face to look at the fire. "If I am a product of your mind, then my thoughts must also be yours, and to seek to express them is irrelevant. If, on the other hand, it is you who are an invention of my own brain (an alternative which I much prefer), then what reason is there for you to deny the very person who gives you life? You are a dream which could be ended in an instant, by the merest sound, the slightest disturbance to some greater mind whose sleep brings you into being.

"This castle, the symbol of my wealth and power, is without substance. At night, when I lose consciousness, it disappears. In the morning it rebuilds itself; the perfection of its renewed manufacture being something which I find paradoxical, but must nevertheless reluctantly accept. Each day my library rewrites itself just as Ferguson left it when he died. That different library which he himself imagined, on the other hand, ceased to exist at the moment of his death."

To seek to refute him was useless, and in any case I was forced to accept the truth of what he said. Since everything in this world was manifestly false and without substance, it could only come about through the thoughts of those who brought it into being.

"Did you take Ferguson's wife as your lover?" I asked.

"The Ferguson whom I employed had no wife."

"And what are the studies which Ferguson helped you to pursue?"

"I am engaged," he said, "on an encyclopaedic survey of the inhabitants of other worlds; their languages, arts and sciences. You may read my work if you wish. Perhaps it would amuse you."

I was not surprised to discover in the printed volume which the Duke indicated to me the words of Magnus Ferguson.

"You are stealing his work and passing it off as your own. You employed Ferguson to write a book which you would publish under your own name."

He said, "If that is what you wish to believe then I shall not anger you by denying it. By being published, any author's words cease to be his own, but rather belong to his reader. Magnus Ferguson renounced all rights over his thoughts once they took life outside his own mind."

I read:

Mars

In the predominant language of this planet, everything is perceived as an object; its actions, relations or attributes causing it to be regarded as a new object, requiring a new name. Thus, for example, a phrase such as "the bird flies" would become "flying-bird"; a noun distinct from "bird". Similarly, the phrase "the white bird flew over the blue lake" becomes a single object (of which the bird and the lake are components), which has been modified to render it as something past.

This language of objects should be contrasted with its main rival in popularity on this planet; a second language constructed entirely from relations. To the speakers of the relation-language, a concept such as "towards" is perfectly meaningful, while to the speakers of the object-language it is incomprehensible. The latter people would, however, understand "towards the sea" as a kind of "sea". For the other tribe, "the sea" would be meaningless until it was presented in relational form, for example as being approached or seen.

Among the minority languages of this world, there are some interesting cases. One consists entirely of smells, secreted by special glands, while another is produced by moving stones in a particular way. (Our own method of communicating, by causing certain vibrations in the air, or else by making visible marks, is surely just as strange). The grammar of these languages is imponderable, but another which has proved amenable at least to partial comprehension is believed to consist entirely of abstract concepts. Amongst those people, the idea that a stone, say, has any existence or meaning independent of its observer is regarded as absurd; one can only speak of "my stone", "the stone I believe that I see" and so on. The difficulty of translating such a language is immediately apparent if one considers the problem of explaining our own concepts. We can, for example, translate a word such as "pride" into all other human languages (though the concept may shift slightly in meaning). To explain it to an alien culture having no knowledge of human society would be an impossible task.

The Duke asked, "Does the passage interest you?"
I told him that his notion of a language in which every concept was abstract and subjective seemed particularly appropriate to the world in which he himself was writing. He frowned when I told him this, saying that he did not know which part of the text I was referring to. I showed him the words I had just read, he looked at them closely and told me that they were an account of the manufacture and dyeing of certain fabrics. I read further:

Jupiter

The beings who float above this great planet have no concept of solidity, or of an "object" as distinct from its surroundings. Their idea of number is derived not from counting, but rather from the perception of ratio and proportion.

The situation is analogous to our own sense of musical pitch. If the frequency of a note is doubled it will be heard to have risen by the interval we call an octave. The beings perceive physical ratios by some other kind of sense, and it has provided them with a way of recognising their environment. The chief feature of their surroundings is the disc of the planet which they orbit, seen as a circle far below. The ratio of the circumference of this disc to its diameter is a quantity which they perceive as a kind of octave; a reassuring chord which distinguishes their world from the space which surrounds it. This ratio (which we know as π) is the basis of all their arithmetic.

The number one is recognised by them as the ratio of their planet's circumference to itself (the idea that their planet is "one" is to them a logical absurdity, the coloured bands which swirl constantly across its face suggesting an ever-changing multiplicity of forms, out of which no unity may be derived). Two is the ratio of the diameter of the planetary disc to its radius, while three is perceived as a profound relation between the volume of their planet and the surface area which must be traversed as they orbit it. As for the number zero, this is sensed by them as the ratio of their world to the entire universe, an ever-sounding drone at the root of their existence, which has tinged their art with a gentle note of despair. All other numbers are expressed as sums of powers of π; the discovery of the infinite expansions of whole numbers greater than three reflecting the famous crisis of the Pythagoreans in our own world. These integers are perceived by them as a series of discords, and consequently were banished from their art at an early stage. The apparent mathematical vindication of their instincts, however, has only encouraged the use of them by some mischievous authors, intent on producing a literature founded on the most sour of juxtapositions.

This section (of which I understood very little) was, the Duke explained, concerned in fact with various questions of engineering, and in particular the methods used in mining certain ores. I could no longer believe that such abstruse material could possibly be the product of my own imagination (unless, that is, my mind contains regions which are far more intellectually advanced than those portions of which I am aware). It seemed that perhaps Magnus Ferguson (the other Ferguson) really did exist, that he had invented a cosmography which took one form in my own perception, and another in that of the Duke. He had written a book which every reader would comprehend in an entirely different manner; what seemed to me to be a passage of mathematics became for the Duke a treatise on mineralogy. Or else perhaps the Duke's plagiaristic rewriting of Ferguson's work amounted to such a drastic reinterpretation of its contents that they became truly his own, at least within his own subjective reality.

"Tell me now," said the Duke, "where have you come from, and why are you here?"

I thought hard, and now that I tried to summon up the contents of my own memory I found them to be turbid and obscure. Out of the darkness all that rose was Margaret's white skin, invented beneath my lips the previous night.

"I was on a ship," I said, troubled by the difficulty I found in recollecting what had happened. "I was bound for Denmark, and there was a storm. The ship was lost, we all expected to be killed. I believe that if I did not die there and then, I must have been carried by the tempest into some other world, which is where I now find myself."

"That is certainly how Magnus Ferguson described it," said the Duke, "when he wrote the Prologue to his *Cosmography*. He described how the cataclysm propelled him into a voyage among the planets, where he could go in search of higher wisdom."

I turned to the next chapter, in the hope that I might find some explanation of Ferguson's purpose, or of how it was that I came to be where I was. "It is an account of agricultural practices," the Duke explained, as I began to read.

Saturn

I cannot understand the things they tell me here, but I realise that the highest wisdom to which humans can attain is still to these people little better than the wisdom of dogs. I tried to tell them of our art, our science, our culture. They showed interest, but saw nothing remarkable in our insights. Our art and science was a stylisation of our instincts, nothing more. If a dog could write a novel, it would consist of a great deal of barking and snarling, and the wagging of tails. These are the emotions of the dog. Would we be interested in the drama of these emotions? The art gallery of the dogs would be filled with pictures of its species, or of fields good for running in; its music would be the orchestration of its howling song. Would we care for any of it? The history of the dogs would be a story of territory claimed and marked in the manner familiar to all, of fights in alleyways; its heroes would be the best fighters, the most prolific urinators. Is this the history we would choose to teach our children?

The people of this world have their own art, their own science, their own culture; but all of it means nothing to me. The achievements of Shakespeare or Newton are for them like the tricks performed by the beast which rounds up sheep, or one which has learned how to open a door. If they can teach us anything, then it would be a feat comparable with making a dog walk on its back legs. At best, we might look like a comical imitation of our teachers, uncomprehending in our loyal attempts to follow their ways.

Whether these people are good or evil, enlightened liberals or tyrannical despots, mirthful or despondent; none of these things is apparent to me. These people seem benevolent to me, they seem content, but perhaps this is an illusion, and their souls harbour secret anguish and frustrations which are just as invisible to me as those of a father are to his child.

I have travelled far, seen many things, and I have learned only that I know nothing, and must doubt everything. Why should I ever have expected the universe to be comprehensible? Each world I have visited contradicts some other, each reality implies the impossibility of every alternative. Perhaps all is false and inconsistent, the universe itself does not exist except as the distorted reflection of the many-mirrored soul which observes it, and my own life has been no more than a fleeting vision, a figure glimpsed in the ill-defined region between successive images in an endlessly descending multiplicity of reflections, identical yet diminishing, one within the next.

"How long is it since Ferguson died?" I asked the Duke.

"He dies every morning, when I awake and am filled with the pain of his loss. During the night he is reborn in my dreams, and continues his great work. The *Cosmography* is almost ended, but must remain perpetually unfinished if it is to be truly perfect, since all that is complete is inevitably flawed."

"Where are the rest of Ferguson's effects?" I asked.

"They die with him each day," was the reply.

I went back downstairs, and after a while discovered the door to a cellar. Inside I found the artifacts of my life, or of many possible lives, piled high in fetid darkness, like so much rubbish. Papers, letters, clothing. I even recognised my own pipe. In the gloom, I was able to see just how fragile that dream was, which I regarded as my own existence. To remove myself from the world amounted to little more than a rearrangement of furniture, a discarding of certain items which had held such meaning for me, such beauty even, and yet for any other would be utterly without significance. My life, in short, was like a language spoken only by myself, a collection of symbols which I alone could decode.

I went back outside, and remembering the envelope in my pocket, took it out, tore it open and read the letter which it contained.

For the attention of Magnus Ferguson

My dear friend,

Time and typhoid have robbed me of my life. But by imagining the possibility that you, Magnus Ferguson, will read these words, I have made the fact a certainty in some world; that is to say, in one world amongst millions. That you should now dream of the possibility of visiting such a world, however briefly, is a happy coincidence, and our meeting is a cause for celebration.

The disease which kills me leaves a space which you may now inhabit, should you choose to do so. I have dreamt of this possibility, and so it too must become true in the world which is now yours. Do not feel pity for me. Enjoy the warmth of my wife's body; I leave her for you. Enjoy my house, and my goods; they are all yours. My work was left incomplete, but now you have arrived to continue it. Do not regret my death, for I do not regret it. Once you dreamt of it, and hence you made it happen, in the world in which I write. Stay here now, record all the things which you have seen, make this world your home and embrace its unreality. Add your own concluding chapter to the Cosmography, and name it Earth.

I bid you cordial greetings and farewell.

Magnus Ferguson.

TALES FROM RREINNSTADT

I

Goldmann woke in an unusually buoyant mood, for the sun was shining brightly outside, and he was particularly prone to the influence of the weather. Rain produced in him a sense of melancholia, cold breezes evoked anxiety, and snow invariably led him into futile arguments. But today there was sunshine already, and this – he felt sure – was a sign of good things to come.

Goldmann was a jeweller, and had grown wealthy from his business over the years. His size had grown likewise, as had that of his wife, who was beginning to stir beside him. Goldmann looked down upon her warm expanse – that pink amorphous mass – and saw dawning consciousness ripple across her face like waves breaking upon a shore. Her mouth was slowly hinging open with a yawn.

He asked her if she had slept well, and this comment was sufficient to dissolve into nothingness the dream which had, only a moment before, so involved Frau Goldmann's attention. It was a dream which she had resolved (as sleep receded) to remember and return to, as soon as she closed her eyes once more. But then Goldmann spoke to her and everything vanished, so that after only a second she could remember nothing of it – except that it had been quite delightful in some manner difficult to ascertain.

They rose. Goldmann had already decided that he would do no work that day. He had just completed some very lucrative repairs on a necklace and tiara, and felt entitled to some rest. However, he thought it wise to tell his wife that he was to go and see a client in the southern quarter of the city. He would not take a carriage; the walk would be quite agreeable on such a warm and pleasant day. In fact, it was his intention to go (possibly via a tavern or two) to see the Museum, which although incomplete, was at least partially open to the public.

They had breakfast together. They each favoured a

generous meal to start the day, not so as to bring about any reduction in the amount of food which might be required later on, but rather as a precaution against any delay in lunch. Breakfast was prepared as usual by Minne, the maid, who brought to their table a large tray decked with sliced ham and sausage, cheeses and bread. For Goldmann there was also a pot of ale, while his wife had her usual drink of honey and lemon in hot water.

Goldmann took a very special delight in the eating of meat. Vegetable matter was no more than an accompaniment, mere ballast, but meat was the true food of man; its rich variety of textures and flavours an ever-changing evocation of mankind's mastery over the animal world. As he lifted a slice of ham onto his plate, and watched the limpness of the paper-thin section of meat, he imagined the foraging of the pig from whence it must have come; that favourite animal of his, so diligent and clever, and so unfairly despised. His consumption of its meat was an acknowledgement of the pig's right to serve the human table; it was a favour which Goldmann granted. And the meat tore most eloquently between his teeth, as his imagination continued to bring back to snuffling life the loyal beast who had made so generous a sacrifice, that Goldmann and his wife might now enjoy their breakfast.

The sausages likewise evoked other quarters of that trotting mass, knee-deep in mud; only now it was its innards which found themselves magically combined with peppers and seasoning – a most wonderful conjunction between animal and vegetable, the latter staking no claims to individual worth as foodstuff, but rather prostrating itself before the far greater nobility of the meat.

Meanwhile, Frau Goldmann was speaking:

". . . And that must have been round about the time when Heinrich the baker was run over by a cart."

"When was that, dear? I don't remember it."

"Must be at least five years ago now. He's never been the same since."

Goldmann put a piece of bread in his mouth, and found it

to be stale. He called Minne and asked her for an explanation.

"Please sir, there was no bread delivered this morning."

"That's what I was saying dear," Frau Goldmann continued; "he's never been the same since he was hit by that cart. Forgetting to deliver the bread – I really don't know how he stays in business. We had the same problem a few weeks ago."

"I suppose anyone can make a mistake now and again," Goldmann suggested. He had been prepared to scold Minne for carelessness, but for Heinrich he felt some sympathy. In any case, the sun was shining today, and Goldmann had no intention of getting angry with anyone. "Perhaps I'll look in on Heinrich later, when I go out for my walk. To visit the client, I mean."

Frau Goldmann raised her eyebrow, as if she had caught the scent of dishonesty. "Is it a rich client?"

"Oh yes, very."

"A woman?"

"A woman's jewellery, of course, but her husband will pay."

"Necklace, is it?"

"That's right." Goldmann hid another piece of stale bread beneath a folded slice of ham, which rested on its platform like glistening silk.

"Is she young or old?"

"Who, darling?"

"The one with the necklace."

"Oh . . . about average."

"Average, I see. And how old is that?"

"I don't really know, my dear," silken ham tearing and melting now between his teeth, and upon his tongue. He continued to speak with his mouth full. "Fortyish perhaps."

"So young? Well. I hope you have a pleasant day, Goldmann."

"What's that supposed to mean?"

"How do I know that this rich forty-year-old 'client' isn't some paramour?"

"Please, my love, you really sound quite preposterous. And Minne can probably hear us."

Frau Goldmann now raised her voice to something approaching that level which her husband might find painful on the ear. "I don't care if Minne can hear us, or the whole street! If I find out that you're running around with some hussy then believe me, Goldmann, you'll be sorry."

After this unexpected outburst, he continued once more to chew and then to swallow the moist pabulum which had paused motionless within his startled mouth during her sudden and humiliating explosion. Minne came back in, and asked if they would like anything else. Frau Goldmann told her no, while her husband looked down silently at the plate of crumbs before him. He finished his pot of ale, then rose to make himself ready for the day ahead. Sheepishly taking leave of his wife, who smiled back at him in modest triumph, he went to shave.

Minne had left the bowl of water for him. He stood over it, looking into the small mirror set up before him. The razor was in need of sharpening, but it would do. Goldmann watched in his reflection the trails it made across his soapy jaw, like a scythe across a field. When he was finished, he called Minne to attend to the bowl, and watched as she stooped to lift it. Not a pretty girl, but young, and Goldmann would often imagine the things he could do with her if he felt inclined.

Now he was ready to go out into the world. Frau Goldmann had gone to the drawing room, where she would spend the day sewing, receiving visitors and eating cake. Goldmann meanwhile put on his coat, picked up his stick and spent a few more minutes before the long mirror in the entrance passage, making sure that he truly looked his best. His hat would conceal the thinnest area of his grey hair, and in his fine attire he could easily be mistaken for someone considerably younger. Once all was in order, Goldmann opened the door and went down the steps, warmed immediately by the sunshine. Before him, the great city of Rreinnstadt awaited.

Goldmann's house was situated in the northern part of town, an area inhabited by the more prosperous tradespeople and craftsmen. His shop, on the other hand, was to the east in Kenntnerstrasse. He might look in on the shop if he was left with time on his hands, just to make sure that Richard was doing his job, but otherwise there was no need to pay a visit there. He began walking to the left, due south. This would lead him towards the Museum and also, thanks to his quick thinking earlier, in the direction of the mythical client whom he had described to his wife. He could not after all discount the possibility that Frau Goldmann was secretly watching him at this very moment, still doubting his word.

He remembered his intention to look in on the baker Heinrich, whose shop was not far off in Sälzerstrasse. A quick detour took him to the place, which he found to be closed. Goldmann knocked on the door, but received no reply. It was most unusual for Heinrich's shop to be closed like this, especially since there was no notice to indicate the reason. Goldmann tried the door; it was unlocked.

The darkness inside was all the deeper in contrast to the bright sunshine which Goldmann left as he entered the gloomy shop, whose shutters remained closed fast. He paused to let his eyes grow accustomed to the crepuscular scene. On the counter, a few loaves were stacked. Perhaps Goldmann ought to help himself and leave the money – but these were stale; Goldmann tested one with his hand and found it to be no better than the one which had so marred his enjoyment of that most succulent ham earlier on.

Now, from somewhere at the back of the shop, Goldmann thought he heard a low noise; the gentle moaning of a woman. He went where his ears directed, passing through an opening and round a corner into the next room where he saw laid out on a board the corpse of Heinrich, his hands across his chest, in an attitude of heavenly repose. Candles burned over him, and at his side his mourning wife was seated. Hat in hand, Goldmann took a spare chair (there were several), and waited in the hope that Frau Heinrich might notice his presence. But she seemed lost in grief.

Poor Heinrich! He looked, in fact, rather healthier in death than ever he did while alive. Death had lifted from his countenance the sorrowful aspect which had hung over him ever since that unfortunate encounter with a milk cart some years earlier. The grey lines and shadows were erased; his face – though pale and somewhat wax-like in appearance – seemed content and satisfied with whatever state it was, in which he now existed. His hair, also, was better combed than Goldmann had seen in a long time. All in all, death had taken years off him, and suited him extremely well.

A man now entered, who shook Goldmann's hand and sat down beside him. "A great loss to the baking profession," he said.

"Indeed," Goldmann replied. "If only I had known that yesterday's bread would be his last, I would have brought out the foie gras for it. As it was, I squandered it on a second-rate bratwurst."

"That is truly unfortunate, though I'm not entirely sure that I would agree with your choice of foie gras. For some of his earlier loaves perhaps – the sort of thing he did twenty years ago. But his latest works were of a kind which only plain butter can adequately complement."

"I can tell that you are quite a connoisseur."

"I am Marcus, brother of the deceased. I was closely involved throughout his career. I was, if you like, a sort of impresario to the theatre of his oven, while he was its Shakespeare."

"He certainly was a most gifted practitioner of his art."

"But also an endless experimenter, who sometimes needed a certain degree of direction. If it hadn't been for me, he would have ended up making baguettes and brioches, and put himself out of business altogether."

"Is that so?" Goldmann kept his voice low out of respect for Heinrich's widow, who made no response to their conversation.

"Certainly. In his early days he was very heavily influenced by the French – their bread was all that counted, our own kinds mattered nothing to him. I grant you, the French do have in their native styles much that is of interest, but fundamentally their palates are very different from our own. But try telling that to my brother! It was all French-this and French-that, Burgundy wines and Roquefort. He even started to learn the language."

"Good Lord, I had no idea."

"And I think he imagined opening some kind of restaurant in Rreinnstadt. It was all madness."

"Was this anything to do with the milk cart

"Oh no, it was long before that – at the very beginning of his career. Everyone must have artistic influences while they find their own manner, but he really was taking things too far. Anyway, things wore off – I like to think it was through my persuading, but it may all simply have been a phase which he had to pass through."

"Was that why you reacted as you did to my foie gras?"

"It merely evoked a memory – a fond memory now, I must say – of my brother's youthful impulse."

"Your father was also a baker, was he not?"

"Of the most traditional kind, so that he gave us both a very thorough grounding in technique. But after a few years of it I knew that a life of dough and yeast was not for me. I went to Mennlingen and initially joined a shipping company; my contact with my brother for the rest of his life was solely by mail."

"I confess I wasn't even aware of your existence, though I knew your brother for years."

"He was the real baker in the family. After his French period he began doing his mature work, around the time that I left Rreinnstadt. In his correspondence he would tell me of his excitement as he experimented with new combinations of grains. And I would always remind him that in the end he had to earn a living, and that maybe the public still wasn't ready for the more exotic areas of his output. Even so, I frequently had to send money in those days to keep him afloat.

"But gradually things took off; he found a style which would satisfy his customers as well as his own sense of artistic integrity. I organised a transportation network to deliver his bread all over the region – he was no good at anything like that. The typical scatter-brained genius, never a clue as to how much money he had or how much he might make."

"Such a quiet chap," said Goldmann; "I didn't realise quite how great his talent was. Though he did strike me latterly as being somewhat disappointed with life."

"He became disillusioned, it's true. Tastes were changing, and his own style came to seem a little out of date. Reviews in the *Almanac of the Baking Industry* went downhill after a disastrous concoction of millet and pumpkinseeds. And then there was the accident."

"The milk cart?" Heinrich's widow gave a flinch as Goldmann said this, as if a painful wound had been reopened. The dead man's brother lowered his voice before continuing.

"He never could believe that it really was an accident at all – he blamed jealous rival bakers. And I wouldn't put it past some of them – I know what a cut-throat profession it is. But whatever the true story, the blow to his head affected his personality quite adversely – his letters became strange and often quite disconnected. I considered abandoning my interests in Mennlingen and coming back to look after him, there being no question of his leaving Rreinnstadt. But I had a family to support and, well, you know how it is."

"Indeed I do, sir, indeed I do. Ah, such a sad loss. And to think that only a short while ago I was eating the stale remnants of one of this man's final masterpieces. Thus do pass all the glories of this world, do they not?" Goldmann stood up. "I trust his end was a peaceful one?"

At this, the widow broke out into a wail of such a heart-rending nature that it made Goldmann truly regret his words. Marcus suggested that the two of them step out into the shop, and then he explained, "It was a final bid to regain his former reputation in the baking world. He was experimenting with a loaf incorporating a new kind of flour derived from wild fungi, and unfortunately he collected a rather deadly species. Had he sold any of the loaves he could have killed half of Rreinnstadt."

Goldmann gave a start. "And are you sure that he didn't sell any?" Already he could feel a strange queasiness, an outbreak of perspiration on his forehead.

"Absolutely. He was too much of a professional ever to sell a product without thoroughly testing it on his own palate first."

Goldmann heard this with some relief. Then Marcus said, "Before you go; may I ask, did my brother ever show you his studio?"

Goldmann told him no, and so Marcus invited him to come back, past the room in which Heinrich's corpse lay at peace, and through another door. In this room, cold now as a mortuary, Goldmann saw the great pair of ovens whose wheaten fruits had given so much pleasure over the years. And beside these, a row of smaller ovens in which Heinrich would conduct his experiments, like some obsessed alchemist. Around the walls, jars and bottles bore labels revealing their contents to be every kind of cereal imaginable, every variety of seed and husk, of pith and pulp. Grindstones of various sizes, and moulds – and even, on a table, plaster models of loaves.

"He always liked to plan everything to perfection. See – here are his sketchbooks." Several volumes filled with nothing but the most exquisitely drawn breadforms in all variety of shapes and textures – even an extensive project, spread over several pages, to design a loaf in the form of a sailing ship. "He only ever made the tiniest fraction of what he saw in his dreams. But such is art."

Goldmann marvelled over the exquisite sketches which his humble baker friend had left behind. All this labour, over mere bread! Were all bakers actually like this; absorbed and obsessed by their work – engulfed by their own vision? Heinrich had been so quiet (so moody – suddenly Goldmann saw him as a very different character). There had been no outward sign of the compulsion which had driven the man.

Goldmann said he was grateful that Marcus should have done him the honour of inviting him into this inner sanctum of the bread-maker's art, but that now he had better leave. As he went back out towards the door of the shop, Goldmann saw again the pile of old loaves on the counter, and the twinge he felt was one of regret alloyed with hunger.

"We shall miss him dearly," he said. "But now I suppose I'd better remember to stop off at Herr Moser's later on to put in an order. Artists have their day, but life must go on."

Goldmann went back out into the bright street, and continued on his way. Such a pity that he would have to find a new source for his morning bread. And if only he had realised before just what craftsmanship lay behind the food he had been eating. He tried to recall it now in his mind, its taste and texture, and to compare it with the work of lesser men. As he considered the matter more closely, he began to identify those areas which may have distinguished Heinrich's work as being that of a genius. There was a uniquely light quality in his output; an apparent superficiality which enabled it to accompany most perfectly whatever meat or cheese Goldmann cared to put on it. Moser's bread could never provide an adequate substitute. And to think that Goldmann had known this man, spoken with him on an almost daily basis, for years! Perhaps he should write a short memoir.

He walked on, and a little later noticed a beggar sitting against a wall. As Goldmann passed, the beggar spoke.

"Spare something for a veteran of Brunnewald."

This made Goldmann stop and turn to inspect the man, whose rags may once have been some kind of uniform, though it was impossible to tell. "You were at Brunnewald? That was a very long time ago, was it not?"

"I was a boy then, sir."

"But you still can't be old enough . . ."

"My looks don't do justice to my advanced age. I was at Brunnewald as surely as I sit here before you now."

"And have you been begging on this basis ever since?"

"I fought in many others, sir, but Brunnewald has turned out to be the most financially rewarding, on account I suppose of it being so long ago. I can raise a few pennies from

Herringen and Mülnau; Knörrenbruck on the other hand is a dead loss. No-one gives you anything for having fought in that one."

This was hardly surprising, such was the humiliating defeat which was suffered there. Goldmann felt generous today; generosity being a peculiar kind of self-flattery in which it pleased him occasionally to indulge. He searched in his purse, and asked the beggar about his recollections of the great battle.

"I was a powder lad with an artillery squadron – though I nearly didn't make it to the battlefield." The beggar was keen to recount his story. "We'd marched all day and were looking for a good place to strike camp for the night when we came upon a farm. The Lieutenant took me to see if there was anyone at home, and when we knocked on the door it was answered by a young girl not much older than myself. She let us in, and gave us both food. She was called Lise, and lived there with an old woman who was deaf and almost blind."

"Go on," said Goldmann, "this is most interesting."

"Well, we had our fill while the rest of the squadron was billeting in the barns, and then the Lieutenant said it was time for us to retire. He took a room upstairs while I . . ."

"Slept in the scullery?"

"Just so, sir. Fancy you guessing it so quickly. Anyway there I was – went out like a light, I did. Then in the early hours of the morning I was woken by an almighty noise."

"You were under attack?"

"Not exactly. There was a commotion upstairs, and I heard the Lieutenant cry out. When I ran upstairs, I came upon the horrible sight of him lying with his own sword thrust into his chest, while the girl stood over him, stained with his blood.

"I was amazed that a frail young girl like that should even have the strength, let alone the inclination, to bring down an army officer, and I wondered what on earth the Lieutenant had done to deserve such a fate. But Lise told me to remain calm – she could see that I was shivering with terror – and explained the reason for her actions.

"Soon after she had gone to bed, she had heard the Lieutenant knocking on her door, asking to be let in. She imagined that he wanted to sleep with her, and refused to allow him inside. But he pleaded that he only wanted to speak with her, if she would dress and come out to see him. So eventually she stepped out to hear his words.

"He said that from the moment he saw her he was struck by the uncanny resemblance she bore to a girl he had known years before, when he himself was a lad. In fact, it was the first girl with whom he ever fell in love. She was the daughter of a farmer, and they used to come and sell vegetables in the village square. One night the young Lieutenant (as he would later become) dreamed that he was in a strange house. He wandered about in it until he found the girl in a room. She was sitting in a rocking chair, and when she saw him she stood up and put her arms around him. They began to kiss and claw at each other most frantically, and he tore at her clothing not knowing quite what he might find – since he had never before seen the naked body of a woman – and as he pulled her dress up he was surprised to find on her belly a most curious mark, like a bruise, so that he thought she had been punched. But the girl said that she had always borne it, and it was a sign of great luck. Then he woke up. Later in the day, the Lieutenant learned that the farmer's daughter had been stabbed to death the previous night.

"The Lieutenant stood telling Lise all of this, and said that she was so similar to the girl he had seen years before that he felt she had to be her reincarnation. So now the Lieutenant wanted to know if Lise also bore a mark. She said she didn't, but the Lieutenant wasn't satisfied; he needed to see for himself. After some futile pleading, he finally grabbed hold of her and said he'd find out by force. Faced with such an assault, you can see why she took hold of his sword and threatened him with it. He took this as little more than a joke, and made a grab at her – but that's how he found himself dead on the floor."

"What an extraordinary story," said Goldmann, "and so like one I once read somewhere . . ."

"But then there was a banging downstairs at the front door. It was some of the other men from our squadron wanting to talk to the Lieutenant. It was a very sticky situation – they'd never believe a girl could do a thing like that, and I'd as likely be hanged for it. She said we'd have to hide, so we went into her room . . ."

"And got under the bed?"

"Of course – where else was there? We only just fitted in the space – real snug it was – and we heard the soldiers break in and find the body of the Lieutenant. They went and woke up the old woman, who hadn't heard a thing of course, and they decided that I must have escaped with the girl after committing the terrible murder. We were under the bed hearing all this.

"Suddenly there was a lot of commotion outside. An enemy division had found our camp and started an attack. Everyone ran out, and Lise and I lay in each other's arms while the battle raged. Our regiment was wiped out – those who survived ran off into the woods and were never seen again.

"But for the rest of the night we stayed in our hiding place, and as our fear left us we began to feel comforted by each other's bodies. I'd never lain so close to a girl, and her soft skin and her gentle breath made me feel hot with desire. At last we started kissing and fondling each other, and in that way we passed the rest of the night. But the remarkable thing was that as I lifted her shift up over her head, I saw on her belly . . ."

"A birth mark?"

"Just so. However did you guess? Though she wouldn't say anything about it. Then next day I walked to Brunnewald, the only survivor of my regiment, and was received by another brigade as a great hero."

"And I believe that there is a further part of your story that you haven't yet told me," said Goldmann. "For was it not the case that as you lay in those cramped conditions underneath the bed, the pressure of contact between your bodies left some lasting mark on yours?"

"I don't believe it did, sir."

"And did she not at some point dig her nails into your skin so that you would have cried out had you not feared being discovered?"

"Not that I can recall, sir."

"And did you not perhaps tell your story years later to someone else, who may have passed it off as their own?"

"Of course, sir; I've told it to many people over the years."

"I do believe," said Goldmann, "that not only is your memory slightly imperfect concerning those events which occurred so long ago, but that moreover you have been left with a memento in the form of a most singular scar upon your buttock."

"Why, whatever might give you that idea?"

"Because I have come across your story elsewhere. Now don't deny it; you may feel slightly embarrassed about it but I know the mark is there."

"I assure you it is not."

"Then kindly prove that to be so by showing me your buttocks."

"Here in the street? What a strange suggestion to come from a gentleman such as yourself."

"Very well, let's go into that side street."

"I assure you, sir, there is no mark."

"In that case why won't you let me verify the fact? Here — one crown if you will show me."

"Certainly not, sir. I may be a beggar but I am an honest soldier and a decent man."

"Two then, if you will only accompany me into that alley and show me your buttocks."

"I'll do it for three."

And so the two of them went to the alley, and once well away from the gaze of the street at large, the old fellow dropped his breeches while Goldmann looked closely to see if there was any mark. And this was when Goldmann felt a hand upon his collar, and turned to see a smartly uniformed sergeant of the City Guard.

"I must ask you both to accompany me to the Fremmelhof."

It was a highly compromising situation in which to be discovered, and all attempts at excuses were fruitless. Leading the two back to the street, the sergeant waved down a carriage and then escorted them to the great fortress which serves both as a barracks and as a prison.

II

From the outside, the building shows little indication of what may lie within its uniform and monotonously grey walls. Small barred windows, high and evenly spaced, are the only means by which the light and air of day are permitted to enter. And it was with a heavy heart that Goldmann was brought, with the old beggar, through the sombre gate beneath those massive walls and then into a room where they were both made to stand before an Officer at his desk. The Officer was a thin and unhealthy looking man, with a sallow complexion, and black hair greased and combed so as to accentuate the form of his skull. Goldmann tried to explain: "It really is a most unfortunate misunderstanding. An accident . . ."

The Officer ignored him, read the charge sheet he had been given, then looked sternly at Goldmann. "It is no accident that you find yourself in this place. You are here because, I understand, you were acting indecently in the streets of Rreinnstadt, and if you were acting indecently then this was because you are of an indecent character, which is in turn a result of your poor upbringing, your unsavoury habits, and the bad company you keep. I am sorry to see you here but not surprised, since your presence means you are a criminal and as such fully deserve to stand before me and feel the full weight and force of the law upon you. Do you have anything to say?"

Goldmann was taken aback by this. "If my being here is so inevitable, then can you also tell me the inevitable outcome?"

"Not yet. I shall have to know the full facts before I can decide how you should be dealt with. But what of you, old man?" he was looking at the beggar. "What's your story?"

"I was already explaining it to the gentleman here," said the beggar. "I had walked all day and I reached the field of Brunnewald, just in time for the battle. I had lost all of my regiment, and joined another with which I fought quite valiantly, though I say so myself. But towards the end of the day I caught a bullet in the leg."

"A bullet," said the Officer, "which had, so to speak, your name on it?"

"You could say that. And so I was put in a cart and taken to the surgeon who said straightaway that my leg should come off immediately. When I heard this I wept and cried at the thought of losing the leg that was so dear to me (it was my favourite, in fact, though the loss of the other would have been little better) and I begged him to spare it. But he said that if he didn't amputate then I would surely die of gangrene; he'd stake his reputation on it. I said my leg was worth more than his reputation, and I'd take my chances. So for several days I was in a hellish fever, at the end of which the wound began to heal."

"And what," said the Officer, "am I supposed to make of all this?"

"Only that if it was ordained that I should catch a bullet in the leg that day then it was also ordained that I should recover. And if it was an accident that I got shot then it was pure chance that I survived. Either way, there was nothing I could do about it."

The Officer was not pleased. "You shall both be put in the cells while I make up my mind what to do with you." And with that, he ordered them to be led away. How strange, Goldmann reflected, that his day out should have taken such an unfortunate turn for the worse!

The cell they were put in was small and damp. "Perhaps it was ordained that we would find ourselves here," observed the beggar, "or perhaps it came about quite by accident. Whichever is the case, there's not an awful lot we can do about it now, is there? But tell me, sir, why were you so sure that I should have a mark on my backside?"

Goldmann explained, "It was because of a story I once read, in an account of the life of a nobleman named Count Zelneck. He is said to have had a servant called Pfitz who told a similar tale concerning his own father, so that when I listened to you in the street I began to wonder if you might be that very man, or even his reincarnation. Pfitz's father lay with Lise beneath the bed, and the pressure of her nails left him with a permanent mark on his behind. The story is so similar to yours that I find it difficult to believe that it is just a coincidence. In fact I suspect that you simply read the story, which is probably false anyway, just as I did."

The beggar cried, "Ah sir, I am found out. Please, don't think ill of me – I am no malicious deceiver. My own father told me the story, though I doubt that he was ever really at Brunnewald either. By retelling it, I'm simply following a kind of family tradition. For you see sir, I am Pfitz."

"How extraordinary," said Goldmann. "I was sure the character was an invention of Count Zelneck's biographer. Yet here you are, large as life."

Pfitz nodded sadly. "Since the death of the Count so many years ago I've had to live by my wits alone. I have no citizenship here in Rreinnstadt, no rights. No-one would employ me, or give me shelter. Officially, I don't even exist."

"What an unfortunate situation in which to find yourself."

"I've grown used to it over the years. But how I miss the Count, and our happy times together! I used to tell him stories to pass the time, and now I have to sell them to survive."

"You've written them down?"

"Oh no, sir; I simply tell them to passers-by like yourself, for a crown or two."

"Well," said Goldmann, "since we may be in here for some time, why don't you tell me one now?"

"Would you like a one crown story or a two?"

"Make it a one-and-a-half."

And so Pfitz decided to tell a story which is most commonly called the Legend of the Tower:

In the Cities of the South, the King and his wife had as their only child a daughter, who cared little for the splendour of the palace. Instead, the Princess preferred to spend her time in an annexe more fit for servants, where she would pass her days reading, or gazing down into the garden below.

In this way she soon came to notice the young gardener. One evening he sang beneath her open window, she went down to join him, and they spent the night together beneath the stars. They continued meeting every night in the garden where they would exchange furtive caresses, until the occasion when they were discovered by a palace guard.

The King, being just and merciful, agreed to spare the life of the gardener, commanding instead that he be flogged and banished. The Princess, meanwhile, swore never to leave her simple home in the annexe, and so the King ordered the window to be bricked up, so that she would remain unseen by men.

The following morning, she watched while the workman set about his task, piling bricks and mortar where her window had been, and she heard the cruel lash of the whip down below. As soon as the workman was gone, she began to scrape with her fingers at the sticky mortar around one of the bricks, until she was able to get a good grip. Then she gradually worked it from its place, until she could look out again; but the garden was empty now. She wiped the brick clean, so that it would remain loose, and pushed it back into position.

Later that day, her maidservant came and handed her a note: *They have given me a good horse and enough food and water to get across the desert. Now I must go. I shall love you always.*

The first few weeks were particularly miserable. The Princess would speak to no-one, remaining in the gloomy seclusion of her cell while the maidservant brought meals which went uneaten, and messages from the King and Queen which she left unanswered. Every evening the Princess would slide the loose brick from its place and look down sorrowfully at the quiet garden. Then one day there was another message, a note which had been found pinned to a tree outside the palace gate:

I rode far today, but now I have stopped for the night to rest my horse. I am following the caravan route to the Cities of the North. I shall leave this letter here with instructions to whoever may find it that it if he is travelling south he should take it and fix it on the tree by the palace. Perhaps one day you will read this. If so, then expect further word from me. Good night.

When the Princess read this it made her very happy. Then afterwards she felt even worse than before, so she read it again. She spent the rest of the day studying the words, the handwriting, the folds in the paper, the patterns of dirt and smudges. In the middle of the night, she awoke to check a part about which her memory was imprecise.

The maidservant was given instructions to go out every day to the tree by the gate; at first being ordered to carry out the inspection seven or eight times a day, then gradually less. After a few weeks a routine was settled into; the maid went first at sunrise, and then again at sunset. No messages were found.

Six months after the beginning of the Princess's self-imposed incarceration, the maid came one morning with a tattered scrap of paper:

My love, the second day has passed. Today I have seen more of the desert; an endless, unchanging and terrible place. The way ahead seems no different from what lies behind me, and vultures have been my only companions. But tomorrow I should come within sight of the Cities of the North, and my sorrow is eased by hope. Now I shall leave this note in the hope that some trader may one day find and deliver it.

As the months passed, the visits from the Princess's mother grew more infrequent, while those from her father ceased altogether. The first year went slowly, the second was much quicker, and many more soon passed, hurried on by the emptiness of the days. Beyond the Palace walls, rumours and stories spread about the strange hermit. Some said she was a wise and saintly person who had shunned the sins of the world in preparation for the end, others that she was a witch who had been locked up because she could not be killed. The Princess's isolation eventually caused her mother to lapse into an incurable sorrow which brought her life to an early end, and then the Princess was left in peace, regarded as deranged by all except her maid, who still continued her twice daily visits to the tree, and found nothing.

Twenty years passed. The Princess, alone and forgotten, drew wisdom from her reading, as she watched her body blossom and fade. Then word reached the Palace that in the Cities of the North there had been a bloody revolt; members of the royal guard had killed the king and seized power. Now a great army had been assembled, which was marching south across the desert intent on conquest. The faithful maid brought ample supplies of food, and joined the Princess in her cell, barricading the door as best she could.

A few days later the attack began. In their dark prison, they listened to the battle outside. The Palace walls were breached; they heard horses and the war-cries of the enemy. They could only guess at the fate of the King and his court. Meanwhile they themselves went unnoticed, and unharmed.

The noise went on for three days and nights, and then there was silence. At last the Princess dared to look out, carefully sliding the loose brick from its place. She blinked in the sunlight as she brought her face close to the gap so as to see as much as she could of the garden. Where the trees had been, she saw only corpses picked by birds. Then she heard the sound of broken glass being trodden underfoot, and strange voices. Men were walking down below. The Princess moved back a little so as to hide her face in shadow, and she saw two men walk into view; enemy officers of high rank. The younger one, slightly built, was wearing the robe of her father. The two men inspected the scene; the young commander pointing this way and that, giving orders. Then he raised his eyes towards the bricked-up window with its tiny opening, and the Princess felt his eyes meet hers. She froze in terror, sure that he must have seen her. His face was young, and seemed almost kindly. Despite her terror she knew again, for the briefest moment, a thrill she had felt years earlier, when she had first seen the gardener. Had she been spotted? But then the two walked away out of sight, and she breathed again.

For another three days and nights there was no sign of life outside. The invaders had moved on. At last their food ran out, and the Princess and her maid left the safety of their cell. They went out into the garden of the destroyed Palace, where the Princess had last stood more than twenty years before. They walked through the remains of the town, and joined the survivors who were quietly rooting for scraps of food.

For several weeks there was anarchy and near starvation, until the conqueror sent an official to govern. Rebuilding was commenced, and the Princess and the maid began new lives as washer-women, their past a closely guarded secret. They stayed together in a simple house near the site of the demolished palace, now a wasteland where wild plants grew. A new generation was born to replace those who had perished, and the Great Lion – for so their conqueror was known – died suddenly during one of his campaigns; some said of poisoning.

The rest of their days went peacefully, though their work was hard. The maid died in her eightieth year, leaving the Princess alone with her memories. Shortly before she too passed away, the Princess went to collect some linen from the house of a wealthy official who happened to notice her, and summoned her to his quarters.

"I am writing a chronicle of the Great Campaign. You are old enough to remember that time, and I wondered if you had any stories of heroism which I might be able to use."

The Princess hesitated. "I don't know, sir. It was a long time ago. Thirty years or more."

The official seemed a little impatient. "Look, this is the sort of thing I mean." He lifted an ancient and tattered scrap of paper. "This letter was found recently in the desert. It must have been written by a soldier to his beloved. A simple thing, but it helps bring history to life. Perhaps you were in love with a soldier?"

She was trying to see what was written on the paper. "Ah, yes, sir. Yes, I was in love. With a soldier. After the city was taken I was hiding in the ruins when he saw me. I was frightened at first, but he seemed gentle and kind."

"Very good. Let me fetch some paper to write this down. Wait here."

As soon as the official left, she picked up the letter. The handwriting was faded by half a century of desert heat, but still familiar:

The third day of my journey has ended. Already in the distance I can see my destination. Tomorrow I shall be there. Fate has ordained that our lives shall be spent apart, but in death we will be together again.

When the official returned he found the old woman waiting patiently, as he had left her. "Now," he said, sitting down, "what was this soldier like?"

"He was very brave, sir, and very kind. But he had to go away with the army."

The official scribbled as she spoke. "Yes, go on."

"So he left. But we swore always to remain faithful to each other, until the end."

"Is that it?"

"That's all I have to say."

"I see." The official sounded weary. "Thank you, anyway. You can go now."

She collected the laundry and went on her way. The basket was difficult and heavy, but her heart was light as she walked over the bridge as usual. In the middle she stopped, and emptied the basket into the river below. She watched the bright pieces of linen fold and twist as the current bore them away. Then she went home, lay down, and died peacefully in her sleep.

On the fourth day, the gardener reached the Cities of the North. He rode slowly through the foreign streets, where the strangely clothed people spoke with unfamiliar accents.

The desert had left his throat dry, his stomach empty. He took his fill at an inn where he saw a pretty serving girl, who asked him where he was from, and why he was so sad. He showed her some coins, and she took him upstairs. Later, he wept on her bosom, lamenting the innocent Princess he had left behind, and cursing her father who had punished him so. Then he saddled his horse and set off again, in the direction of the most remote region of the land, where the people live a simple life of agriculture, and he was never heard of again.

But the serving girl was left with something to remember him by. Nine months later she gave birth to a son; a small, weak child, born with the cord around his neck so that everyone thought he would die, or grow up an idiot. Yet the boy survived. First they called him the Sparrow, because of his small stature. Then when he was old enough to join the army they called him the Eagle, for his keen eye and his love of killing. Not content with the high rank and honour he soon gained, he led a plot to murder the King, and afterwards had all his fellow conspirators put to the sword, and then they called him the Great Lion, and he raised a vast army and marched it south, laying waste to everything he found.

"Is there a moral to the story?" said Goldmann.

"I prefer to do without morals," Pfitz replied. "I find they only get in the way. But now I'm richer by a crown and a half, and my head is lighter by the weight of one story."

There was still no sign of the guard, or any way that the two prisoners might guess how much longer they would have to remain captive. Goldmann was satisfied that once his own credentials were checked he would be released with an apology, but Pfitz on the other hand might not be so lucky, and already Goldmann had come to feel fond of the beggar. It was to try and calm his own fears for him that Goldmann made his next comment:

"I expect that you must have been in this sort of situation on many occasions."

"Only once, sir. I've done my best over the years to keep out of harm's way. As I'm a non-citizen, it wouldn't do me any good to come to the attention of the authorities. It would upset their paper-work, since I don't exist on any of their lists, and Lord knows how they might decide to patch things up. But a few years ago I did find myself in this very fortress, and in a cell even more unpleasant than this one. It was the time of the Corn Tax . . ."

"That was a great many years ago."

"I can't promise that my memory is entirely accurate, but you can be sure that no matter how imperfect it is, I know the history of my own life better than you, and you'll just have to bear with me."

"You aren't going to tell me another tale of your father's, are you?"

"What difference will it make to you whether the story happened to me or to someone else – or to no-one? It will pass the time, and it won't cost you a penny."

"Very well, go on then."

And so Pfitz continued. It was the time of the Corn Tax – a very unpopular law. Meetings were being held and clubs were formed to debate the issue. Pfitz had no interest in any of it, but quite by chance (or else because it was ordained), he got caught up in a riot.

"It had started out as a peaceful meeting," Pfitz explained, "but then the militia arrived and turned it into a battle. That's what happens when you put boys with guns in charge of grown people. I was only trying to make my way from one end of town to the other, but before I knew it I was in the middle of the mob, and then I felt myself being picked up by two soldiers and thrown onto the back of a cart to be carried to prison."

He was crushed alongside ten or twelve others – men and women – on the cart. After a short but very uncomfortable journey, they arrived at the Fremmelhof where they were marched into a cell. Those who were not quick enough to find a place on the stone benches had to crouch on the fetid slabs of the floor. Some of the prisoners were sobbing, others sat in stunned silence. All feared the worst. Pfitz turned to the man beside him. "Whether we are here by accident or by

Divine purpose, we can be sure that there is no reason in human logic why any of us should now be held prisoner. Why don't you tell me the story of how you came to find yourself here?"

His companion was a sorrowful-looking man, whose head hung low and whose sadness seemed to exceed even the dismal bounds of his present condition. He said his name was Schmidt, and then told his story:

"Hannah and I met when we were each just fifteen years old, and we fell in love immediately. She was a sensitive, intelligent girl, still saddened by the death some years earlier of her mother (a fine woman, by all accounts). Her father, on the other hand, was a bad-tempered fellow who immediately showed his disapproval of me, though my means were not inadequate. He banned me from seeing Hannah, but realised that the time had come when he had to get her safely off his hands. A coal merchant named Holzmann had a son of the right age, and this seemed like a good catch. Never mind that the indolent youth was horribly pock-marked and so thin he looked as if the wind might blow him away; his father's wealth was what mattered.

"Hannah, of course, was horrified by all this – even more so when she actually met the unfortunate chap, who stuttered and mumbled his way through an interview with her. She told me at one of our secret meetings that she would rather die than spend her life tethered to that miserable creature.

"And so we decided that the only hope was to run away together. We didn't have long to prepare ourselves – negotiations were well under way concerning Hannah's fate, and her father favoured an early betrothal. He planned to take her to the country in the meantime, out of harm's way. We would have to make our escape within the week.

"During the next few days I put together what cash I could, and secretly packed my belongings. Hannah likewise made herself ready, until the appointed evening came. I had arranged for us to take a coach from the town square, and I waited in the darkness near her house until she gave the sign for me to go and catch her as she lowered herself from her open window by a rope of knotted bedsheets. Once she was safely down, we hurried to catch the coach.

"That was our first disaster – the coach didn't arrive. I wondered if the driver might have alerted our parents; it seemed unwise to wait there in the square any longer in the hope that it would eventually show up. We would have to find other transportation.

"We walked for an hour or so, through the deserted streets, all her belongings strapped on my back save a small bag which she carried in her hand. It wasn't long before we began blaming each other for the predicament we were in, and only the undesirable prospect of the coal merchant's son prevented Hannah from turning back. But eventually we heard the sound of hooves and cart-wheels – a caravan was coming up slowly behind us. It was driven by an old pedlar who offered to convey us – he and his wife were going to Mittelburg to sell their wares, and this seemed as good a place as any for Hannah and I to start our new life. So we climbed into the back of the covered wagon, and there we found the pedlar's wife cradling a baby, seated in the tiny space that served as their home. There was just enough room for us to get ourselves and our bags inside, and I had to mind my head with all the pots and pans that were swinging from the hooks where they were tied. The woman offered us some of the stew which was boiling over a tiny stove of hot coals in the corner of the caravan, and as we ate I noticed the pile of children's dolls on the floor. These, we were told, were what the couple made and sold. They were simple-looking things, male and female in roughly equal numbers, with crude clothes made from scraps and rags.

"The food and rest, and the simple comfort of the wagon, gave me renewed hope, and I could see that Hannah also had regained her determination to go ahead with our scheme. But our long walk had left us very tired, and we soon needed to sleep. There was a single narrow bed inside the caravan –

Hannah and I lay down on the floor beside it, where we were soon deep in sleep.

"Some time later, I was woken by a strange sound. The caravan was stationary now; in the total darkness, I could hear the steady breathing of the pedlar and his wife in their bed. Beside me, Hannah showed no sign of stirring; while the baby, asleep in its crib, was making no sound. But I was sure that what had woken me was a voice; a very quiet, high calling – like a child somewhere far off. Fully awake now, I lay still and listened in case it might happen again – then I heard it! A tiny voice, calling as if for help, out of the blackness somewhere to my left. I realised that the sound came from the corner where the dolls lay. Could it be that one of them had cried out to me? I reached over, groping for the pile until my hand found a doll which I brought back for examination, careful all the while not to make a sound which might disturb my hosts. I couldn't see the doll which I held, nor did I hear anything when I placed it close to my ear, but as I ran my finger over its face and arms I came to realise that it was not made of wood as I had supposed, but of some other substance; cold and hard, but also porous and very light. It must be made of bone. And at once a terrible scenario became apparent – that these pedlars made their living by murdering people and manufacturing dolls out of them. As for the stew they had served us, who knows what terrible meat it may have contained? My guess was that some time during the night the pedlar would try to slit our throats – perhaps they had already drugged us, since sleep had come so readily. But now I was alert and ready for them, and for the rest of the night I lay vigilant beside Hannah, prepared to thwart any attack.

"However, no such assault was made on us. Morning came, and eventually the pedlar and his wife awoke and asked if we had rested well. We were camped in a remote place which I did not recognise, near a river. The pedlar offered us some bread and ale, and Hannah and I got out of the caravan to stretch our legs. By now, I was prepared to believe that my terrifying theory was wholly false – that I had only imagined the voice in the night. And when I asked the woman how the dolls were made, she said only that they were carved from animal bones.

"We had little choice but to carry on our journey with them – we were in the middle of nowhere. So we sat in the back with the wife and baby while her husband harnessed his horse and took us once more on our way. I asked the woman again about the dolls – did they make many, did they fetch a good price? I still felt an unquenched curiosity and suspicion. She said that she had been taught the art by her mother, who had in turn learnt it from hers – the secret went back many generations. Any old animal bone would do, and the precise manner of carving was not terribly important. What mattered was the final treatment which the dolls received after their completion. We sat in rapt silence in the swaying caravan as the method was explained to Hannah and myself by the pedlar woman. You first had to find someone who was close to the end of life – a sick patient on their death bed, or a criminal being led to the gallows – and you had to take something from them to give to the doll. A hair would do, or a scrap of clothing, but the surest thing of all was the last dying breath – trapped if necessary in a bottle for later use. She then showed us a wooden box, kept beside the pile of dolls, full of small sealed bottles each of which, she claimed, contained just such final breaths, from various people over the years. It was, she explained, a constant supply for use in her work.

"The dolls therefore had a dual purpose. First, they would when treated in the required way absorb all the sins of the donor, that he or she might reach Heaven more quickly, and secondly the dolls would bring to whoever possessed them the watchful eye and guardianship of the departed soul, who might if necessary put in a good word with the forces on the other side.

"I then told her of the voice I had heard in the night, and asked if the dolls did this often. She didn't look at all surprised, but said that what I had heard was not a doll, but rather the voice of one of the bottles. They frequently did this, she said; particularly if the donor had been speaking at the moment of death, so that their voice had become trapped along with the air which was breathed into the vessel. She held one of the bottles close to my ear and asked me to listen carefully; then she gave it a little shake and as she did so I heard stirring within it a tumbling, confused sound, faint and indistinct, which then settled into that high calling I had heard during the night. This was one of the noisiest ones, she explained; from a woman who had recently suffered a painful death. Her breath would soon be ready to be given to a doll, and then her soul – free at last from all evil – would fly into Heaven.

"I would have found all of this quite beyond belief, were it not for the evidence of my own ears. We rode on into Mittelburg, and there Hannah and I bade goodbye to our extraordinary friends. But before leaving us, the woman handed us a doll and told us to keep it for good luck – it was a girl doll, and carried the breath of a child who had died of typhoid before her fifth birthday. This, she assured us, would be an extremely powerful possession, and we must be sure never to harm it.

"Then Hannah and I went to find accommodation, arriving soon at an inn which was clean and affordable. The manager didn't ask too many questions about us, seeming quite willing to believe that we were already married, as long as we paid everything in advance.

"We had every intention of legitimising our relationship as soon as possible; in the meantime, I slept on the floor of our room in the inn, while Hannah occupied the bed. After a couple of days the place looked quite homely, with some flowers which Hannah arranged in an empty wine bottle, on the window-sill a drawing which she had made of her late mother, and – lying on the bed – the doll which we had been given.

"I was seeking work, going round every shop and yard I could find, asking every driver if he needed a mate. It was not easy; I found odd jobs running errands or heaving some bricks, but permanent employment evaded me. A few weeks of this precarious existence began to take its toll on us. We could not be married until I found proper work, and this frustration only added to our problems. One night things came to a head, and we had our first argument. I had never seen Hannah like this, and I didn't like what I saw. We shouted and swore at each other, spat venomous insults, and wholly ignored the bangs of complaint which landed on the walls of our room from disturbed neighbours. Then, at the height of her rage, Hannah picked up the doll and flung it at me. I ducked, it hit the wall, and shattered into several pieces.

"We both went silent. We knew what an ill omen this was. Hannah began to cry, and I went to pick up the pieces of the broken doll. I remembered the dying child who had once breathed life into it, and the thought of that poor suffering girl made me realise how foolish the two of us had been to argue so bitterly, when we should be enjoying life. I embraced Hannah and tearfully asked her forgiveness, and then I pinned the limbs of the doll back in place. Later, with the aid of some flour and water, I would be able to hold together the pieces which had fractured. Hannah and I went to sleep that night with a sense of shame and foreboding.

"Next morning, we were told that we would have to leave because of the noise we had been making. We packed our belongings and went to search for another inn. It was harder now to find somewhere suitable; we no longer looked as fresh and trustworthy as when we had first arrived in Mittelburg, and we were turned away on many occasions. Eventually we had to settle for a shabby place which looked more like a hostel for vagabonds. The noise of coughing and spitting was endless; the thin fabric of the building gave us no protection from the foul conversations in the beer hall below. But our misfortunes were only just beginning. Within a few days, the unclean air of the place had brought about a sickness in Hannah which might easily have been cured had we been able to afford better food and perhaps some medicine. Instead, her condition rapidly deteriorated until she became feverish. I felt sure that the doll was punishing us with ill luck, but I didn't dare destroy it or harm it in any way.

Instead, I kept it wrapped in a soft cloth, in the hope that I might soothe its temper.

"Not long after, I was walking the streets in search of work when I saw a notice pasted to the wall. It was from Hannah's father – the offer of a reward for any information leading to her discovery. The town was no longer safe for us. I went back and began to pack our things – Hannah was still too weak even to get out of bed, but we had to be ready to take flight at a moment's notice. As soon as she was fit enough we would head for the next town.

"The following night, I was woken from my sleep by a knock on the door. I rose from my bed on the floor and quickly dressed, then as I went to open the door I heard the voice of Hannah's father. We had been betrayed! I gathered up all our bags and prepared for escape, which could only be made through the window I now opened. Hannah was in a sleepy daze – I carried her to the window, dropped our bags down to the street below and after crawling out onto the narrow balcony began to pull her after me. The door was being rammed by the people outside – it was a desperate race to try and fit Hannah's limp body through that high narrow window, and onto the ledge outside.

"But already they had broken in; her father, the innkeeper and another huge man. Hannah was only halfway through, her shoulders in my arms. 'What's happening?' she kept asking in her confused state. Then I felt them tugging at her feet to prevent me drawing her out to freedom – it was me at one end against three hefty fellows at the other, and I wondered if poor Hannah might split in two. I had no choice but to abandon her. I leapt down to the street, gathered up what I could carry of our belongings, and ran off. Another inn gave me shelter that night, then next morning I took the coach to Helmbach, cursing our ill luck and the man, Hannah's father, who had shattered all our dreams. At Helmbach, however, things now proved easier for me. I quickly obtained employment at a printer's works, and was able to lead a decent life."

Sitting beside him in the cell, Pfitz had listened intently to Schmidt's words. "And is that the end of your story?"

"My friend," Schmidt had replied, "that was hardly the beginning. While living at Helmbach, I learned of Hannah's fate. She was taken back and married to Holzmann, the coal merchant's son; an event which broke my heart, I can tell you. All I had to remember her by were a few of her possessions, and the doll which I still kept, not daring to harm it, though I held it responsible for all our misfortunes. I longed to return to my home town in order to save her, but her father had sworn to kill me if he ever found me. And so I remained in exile at Helmbach, where I led a peaceful and solitary existence. As for my own parents and family, I could not allow them to know anything of my whereabouts.

"Many years passed. I rose to become a partner at the printing firm, and enjoyed a life of comfort and prosperity. One evening, while walking in the town, I saw a dishevelled young woman squatting at the roadside, a blanket laid out before her. Upon it was a row of bone dolls. I went over and asked her about them; it was, she said, an ancient craft which she had learned from her mother. I realised in the course of our conversation that this must be the girl whom I had seen as a baby, in the arms of the pedlar woman so long ago. I told her my story, and how the doll had brought us such ill luck. Then she put her head in her hands and shook sorrowfully. 'You poor things,' she said, 'and so foolish, to mistreat a doll like that. But had you found my mother again, she would have told you that the simple remedy was for your lady friend to apologise most sincerely to the doll she had hurt, and then all would be put right. For they're very sensitive things, you know – especially ones with child spirits in them. But if she didn't apologise, then all her life she will have had the greatest misfortune.'

"I ran immediately back to my home and found the doll, still kept safely in a cupboard. I knew that I had to go back, whatever the risk, and find Hannah. The following morning I arrived in my home town. My reunion with those of my family who still survived was, you can imagine, joyful beyond words. As for Hannah's father, I learned that he was dead and no longer a danger to me; likewise the coal merchant Holzmann. His son, Hannah's husband, had inherited everything. But when I went to their grand house, I found it abandoned and boarded up. The caretaker told me that the couple who had lived there had suffered a life of misery – each of the four children the lady (Hannah) had borne had died in infancy, while the coal business on which they relied had collapsed in ruins. The two had now moved to a humble rented apartment in the Niedergasse, where they lived by mending clothes.

"After trying nearly every door there, I at last found one which was opened by the pathetic figure of Hannah's husband, emaciated and consumptive, and too weak to show any emotion when he realised who I was. I told him that their salvation had finally arrived, if he would now let me speak to his wife; but he said that this was impossible. He showed me the note which he had found that morning – I still remember its every word. *Dear husband, I have brought you nothing but disaster, and you are better off without me. Hannah*. He had no idea where she went. That was five years ago."

"And so for five years you have been searching for her?" Pfitz asked.

"That is correct," said Schmidt. "I have given up all work other than this single quest. It is an obsession which has taken me through many towns and villages, my path retraced endlessly in the hope that I will one day find her. My most recent visit to Mittelburg was another failure, and so I came to Rreinnstadt to continue my search. I found myself caught up in a riot, and I was arrested, just like you and everyone else here."

"It is a very touching tale," Pfitz said to him, "and told most eloquently. But you must forgive me if I say that I find it hard to believe a single word of it."

"I can understand your scepticism. Perhaps, though, you might like to see the object which has been the cause of everything which took place?"

Then Schmidt reached into his pocket and brought out the bone doll, dirty and ragged. He passed it to Pfitz, who studied it closely. "How fascinating," Pfitz said. "So you really ascribe your fate and that of the woman you loved to this sorry-looking object?"

Schmidt replied that this was what he believed, and nothing would cause him to change his opinion.

Goldmann found Pfitz's story very curious. "What happened to Schmidt? Were you all released?"

"An informer was brought to our cell," Pfitz went on, "claiming to know the ringleader who had started the riot. He pointed to Schmidt. The man was innocent, of course, but the informer had to name someone in order to buy his own freedom. It could just as easily have been me or anyone else in the cell who was condemned, but either it was Schmidt's bad luck or else it was ordained by fate that he would be chosen. Either way, he was the one they hanged."

"My God!" Goldmann was astonished by Pfitz's calm manner. And he began to wonder what outcome might await the two of them, once the guards came.

"But before they led him away, Schmidt gave me the doll and made me promise to look for Hannah. Next day I was released."

"What did you do then?"

"I threw the doll into the river."

Goldmann was outraged. "You disobeyed the request of a condemned man?"

"He never knew anything about it."

"He trusted you to fulfil the quest which he had pursued for so long, and to find the woman he loved."

"She'd probably met someone else and made a respectable life for herself. Even if I could have found her, I would only have made her unhappy when I told her the story. Why increase the suffering of the world for the sake of someone who was no longer even in it?"

"Then what about the doll? Did you not fear its power?"

"I already told you, I found Schmidt's story ludicrous. To spend all those years fretting over a woman is bad enough –

but a doll? And even if it did have any magic quality, then it had hardly been lucky for Schmidt. I wanted nothing to do with it."

Goldmann was not persuaded by these arguments. "I was beginning to like you, Pfitz. But I can see that you have a heart of ice. You are a monster!"

Pfitz was not at all dismayed. "Calm down sir. If it's any comfort to you, I could say that none of it ever really took place."

"Is that so?"

"Does it make you feel better?"

For a long time, neither spoke.

III

It was Pfitz who eventually broke the silence. "How I do miss my master."

"You mean Count Zelneck?"

"We used to have such interesting discussions."

Goldmann sniffed. "And did you tell him outrageous stories as well?"

"Only when it pleased him. But he also taught me about philosophy, and made me read all the masters – though none of them had any answers. We used to argue about whether a man blind from birth, having been given the power of sight, would be able to recognise the world around him without touching it. And we discussed the question of whether an infant raised by animals would acquire speech. And we also used to talk about the people who might live on other planets."

"I've thought about that as well," said Goldmann. It had been one morning, while his wife lay asleep beside him. "Just imagine the strange worlds which might exist up above, and all the wonderful things those people could tell us." Goldmann felt willing to pursue the subject, since it might take his mind off his troubles.

"We'd have to learn their language first," Pfitz said.

"You think that would be a problem?" Goldmann retorted. "I've read a little bit of philosophy too, you know. And according to the latest theories, the natural language which God speaks – and hence our celestial friends also – is German."

Pfitz laughed. "The Germans say that their language is the most natural, likewise the French and English. All it proves is that philosophers are capable of talking more nonsense than a drunken stevedore – except that the philosophers can dress their arguments more elegantly."

"All right then," said Goldmann, warming to the theme, "How do you think it would be, if we were to meet people from another world?"

"Let us try and imagine the scene," Pfitz began. "We are freed from our cell, and are riding together now along a quiet country lane, when we see a great light in the sky, or a cloud, out of which a fantastic vessel descends. It falls slowly to the ground, a door opens – and a puddle of slime oozes out."

"What a disgusting notion," Goldmann said. "But where are our visitors?"

"These are the visitors; these crawling pools of slime. On their planet, the force of gravity is so immense that to stand upright would be an impossibility, and so they are all as flat as a pancake. Having no dimension of height, their only means of motion is through a continual redistribution of their shape."

"But do they have to be so slimy? I haven't had lunch yet."

"If they were not, then friction would make it very hard for them to get around. Now here they are, in a line before us, these puddles of slime from another planet. How shall we greet them?"

Goldmann said, "I confess that the physical form of these visitors has taken me somewhat by surprise. Though I suppose that common courtesy would require me to get down from my horse, take off my hat and bid them good day."

"Is that all? One of them may be the Slime King, you

know. Better get down on your knee to them just in case. And once you've done this, what next?"

Goldmann pondered the question. "I suppose I would await their reply."

"You expect them to speak? I'm afraid their planet has no air, and hence sound is an unknown phenomenon to them. They communicate by rubbing against each other in a highly meaningful way. So how shall we greet our slime friends?"

Again Goldmann thought for some time. Then an idea occurred to him. "I might try rubbing them with my finger, to see whether I can get any response."

"That would probably be impolite, but I agree that the only hope of making ourselves understood is to begin to explore their frictional vocabulary. How shall we do this?"

Goldmann said, "I would approach one of the creatures, and rub it in various ways. With each way, I would observe its response."

"Very well," said Pfitz. "You do this ten times to each of them. Perhaps you've said all manner of things, and perhaps they have tried to respond, but you haven't observed any of it."

"All right," Goldmann replied. "I should look for regularities or patterns in what they say. I might find that there is a certain message which they repeat many times. I would somehow learn to rub this message back to them. It's as if I were to say 'Hello' to a foreigner, and he were to say 'Hello' to me."

"It'll be a long slow business, though, to decode the language of the slime people."

"Slow, but nevertheless possible," Goldmann continued. "A traveller in a foreign land may initially understand nothing, and his hosts may not speak his own language; but after living there for a while, he picks things up bit by bit, and manages to communicate; at first by simply repeating words. It's no different from the way a child learns to speak. And since your slime children must also learn to converse with their parents, I suppose that we shall be able to imitate their efforts and master their language. It may take a long time, but I see no reason why we should not be able to achieve it."

Pfitz nodded in agreement as he heard this, but then raised an objection. "The child, or the traveller, are humans among other humans. Already they share a common language of gestures, urges and instincts, before a single word is uttered. What of the slime people? Their only behaviour, as far as we can make out, is to crawl around."

Goldmann was not to be put off. "One of them might crawl onto a rock, and then communicate a rubbing word with which I would then reply, after indicating another rock. And the creature would use some other word to signify that I was correct in naming that object as a rock."

"How is the creature supposed to know that what you are naming is a rock?"

"Because I point at it."

Pfitz laughed. "And a puddle of slime from another planet is supposed to know that when you extend a limb in a certain direction then you are naming something?"

"Very well, I pick up the stone, or I might even lie upon it, in the same manner as the slime creature."

"I see," said Pfitz. "So you have now learned their word (or rather gesture) which denotes stone. You spend a considerable time finding other stones and agreeing with your new friends that these are indeed stones, whether in your language or theirs. At last, you pick up another rock, no different from the rest, and when you give the creature the gesture for stone it replies with some entirely new kind of rubbing-word."

"What does that mean?"

"I don't know. That's the problem. Were we wrong in naming those other stones as we did? Does this latest one have some property which the others didn't possess? Were the creatures all along trying to tell us that we were wrong, and it is only the last stone which we have named correctly?"

"Perhaps you have a point," Goldmann conceded.

"In decoding their language, we would at each stage be making a great many assumptions, and in order to validate these assumptions we would already have to understand these creatures before we even began the task of trying to learn their vocabulary. We would have to understand their behaviour, their habits, their culture. Only then would we really be in a position to make a start."

"I can see that you are no ordinary beggar," said Goldmann, "and the Count trained you well. But I still can't agree with your arguments about the slime people. If there's any logic to them then surely it must be possible to unravel their language."

"Think of it the other way round," said Pfitz. "If you wanted them to understand our own language, how might we translate words such as 'happy' or 'angry'? Is there any reason why they should mean anything to a puddle of slime?"

"Then perhaps emotions have no real meaning at all. But we could still try, for instance, to find out about their scientific theories. We could concentrate on the logic of their language."

Pfitz thought a while. "I once saw a parrot," he said, "which could speak exactly like a human. It had the voice of a woman, and came out with a great variety of phrases. It could probably even have learned to tell an entire story for all I know. But I did not infer from that behaviour that it was a rational creature, or that there was any meaning behind its actions other than the desire to imitate and hence be rewarded by its owner with another nut."

"Why is this relevant, Pfitz?"

"While you spend so much time trying to decode the language of the slime creatures, you may be observing actions which are automatic and quite without intention. You might get as far as having extended conversations with the slime people (or so you would believe) when in fact their words are empty and devoid of meaning. So how shall we decide whether the slime creatures are rational beings, or whether their behaviour is automatic and instinctive, like that of an ant or a parrot, and hence without meaning to them?"

"You're lost in philosophy, Pfitz. Just think of the world

around you – of the ants you mentioned. How could anyone mistake their behaviour for intelligence?"

"You only 'know' they aren't intelligent because you know that they are ants. How could the slime people, for example, distinguish between the behaviour of the ants in the yard, and that of ourselves?"

"The behaviour of the ants is repetitive and mechanical, ours is complex and varied."

"Then patterned behaviour is a sign of instinct rather than intelligence. The most intelligent behaviour of all might appear completely random. How might the slime creatures demonstrate their intelligence to us?"

"They might use the materials they find around them to build a shelter."

"In the manner of birds?"

"Or they might begin to respond to my words."

"Like a dog?"

"Or show evidence that they were aware of their own existence."

"Like an ape which knows its own reflection?"

"Very well then," said Goldmann. "I suppose that if I wanted to know whether they had the intelligence of humans, I would want to converse with them, and hence perceive that they have thinking minds."

Pfitz laughed triumphantly. "But we've already decided that even if we were to believe ourselves to have decoded their language then this will tell us nothing; we may have invented a meaningful language where none exists, or else their expressions may be instinctive and have nothing to do with the presence of consciousness. It would probably also be true to say that the more intelligent the creatures were, the less chance we would have of understanding them, since their language would be complex and abstract, unlike those creatures which have a language of only two noises, meaning 'go away' and 'I'm here'."

Goldmann sighed. "Then we would have even less chance of talking to them than we do of communicating with the animals around us."

"Just so," said Pfitz. "Unless, that is, I am completely mistaken. But at least our discussion has helped to pass a little more time."

Goldmann was not satisfied with this, but he had had enough of Pfitz's philosophy. "I'm sure your ideas are all stolen from some book or other, just like all your other tales."

"Of course they are, sir. If I'd made up all my ideas myself I'd hardly be likely to give them away to strangers for free, would I? I told you, I've read all the great philosophers, and a good many not-so-great ones too; my master the Count encouraged it. And I also came upon some very interesting material once when we received a visit from a man who had completely lost his memory."

Pfitz described how he was going about his usual duties one morning while the Count was upstairs reading, when there was a loud knocking at the door. Going to open it, Pfitz saw a thin and dishevelled figure, his clothes ragged and dirty:

"We don't want your sort round here. Clear off!"

("You see," Pfitz explained to Goldmann, "this was in the days before I became a beggar myself. My mind has broadened considerably in the intervening years.")

"Clear off!"

"Have pity on me, sir," said the stranger, "all I ask is some water." He was holding out a flask, and looked quite pathetic, so Pfitz softened and led him to the pump. There, while Pfitz pulled the handle, the stranger not only filled his flask but also put his head beneath the spout, drinking the cold water and washing his face and hair.

"Thank you, sir!" He stood up, refreshed.

"You don't talk like a beggar," Pfitz said, "and your accent sounds foreign. Where do you come from?"

The stranger stared at him sadly. "I'm afraid I have no idea. I've forgotten who I am, where my home is, and where I should be going. All I have to assist me is this satchel of papers which I carry."

Pfitz, sensing a good story which might one day prove profitable to him, straightaway invited the stranger inside to rest a while and tell him whatever he could. They sat down together in the kitchen, where the stranger ate some bread and soup which Pfitz provided.

"I believe that I come from a place where there are mountains," the man said, "but I may of course be mistaken. Mountains often appear in my dreams, as does the face of a certain woman, but these could be no more than idle fantasies."

Pfitz nodded sagely, "I sometimes have dreams like that as well."

"Some days ago (I have lost count how many) I found myself lying in a ditch by the roadside. The sun was not long risen and I was woken by light rainfall. My head was sore, and not only had I no idea how it was that I had come to be there, I could not even remember my own name."

"Sounds as though you were set upon while travelling. The robbers must have beaten you unconscious and left you for dead."

"That is one of the theories which I have considered during the last few days, while I have continued along the road on which I awoke; though whether my long hours of walking are taking me in the direction of my appointed destination, or else back to the place from which I came, I cannot say."

"What about this satchel of yours?"

The stranger placed it upon the table. "Yes, this is the only clue which I possess, but it is more diverting than truly helpful. My assailants, if we are to believe in their existence, clearly had no use for its contents." He opened it and drew out a sheaf of handwritten pages. "There is an experiment which I should very much like to conduct," he said. "Could you bring me a pen and ink?"

Pfitz did as he was asked, and the stranger began to write on the blank side of one of the sheets. He then turned it over.

"As I thought. The handwriting is indeed my own, though I still find it unlikely that I am the author of these various documents. In the place from which I come I must have been employed as a copyist."

"If you live by copying alone then the loss of your memory really isn't such a handicap after all," Pfitz said brightly. "But what are your papers concerned with?"

The stranger turned the corners of the pages he held, glancing at the words on them as if reminding himself of something he might otherwise doubt. "These documents, mere fragments from some larger work or series of works, appear to relate to a certain place which I can only suppose to be imaginary; a fantastic city, or else perhaps several cities; an entire world, or even a universe, conceived in a form and detail which one might term encyclopaedic. I have on several occasions wondered whether I myself am a visitor from the impossible city of which my own hand has written, and whether my very existence is therefore a paradox, an illusion."

Pfitz laughed. "You're as real as this table, I can see that with my own eyes. Why don't you let me read some of your manuscript?"

And so the stranger showed Pfitz an 'item concerning something called the Dictionary of Identity.

At its most superficial level, the idea behind the Dictionary is a trivial one. We are all identified by a name – two (first and second) being already superfluous, any more mere vanity. Of course, there are many people who share the same name; the system is made inefficient by the paucity of imagination with which it is applied. If we used numbers instead, then a dozen or so digits would be enough to provide a unique address for every human who has ever lived, or will be born in the next few centuries.

These numbers could be chosen with the same randomness by which individuals currently find themselves named after saints or ancient heroes. But the editors of the Dictionary decided on a far more logical and systematic method.

Their first scheme began by naming Adam and Eve as 1 and 2; each subsequent individual in human history would be numbered chronologically. Naturally, this scheme very quickly ran into severe difficulties. It was hard enough to place the people of antiquity in correct order; greater still was the problem of how to deal with those multitudes of individuals who are not explicitly discussed in ancient scripture. How many unknown people came into the world in that brief moment which separated the births of Jacob and Esau?

Faced with such an enormous obstacle, there were those who sought to surmount it by simply refusing to believe in its existence. These people claimed (and argued the point most vigorously) that the sacred texts made implicit reference to every individual alive at the time (this being no more than yet another manifestation of the divine nature of the work). Their argument was a simple one. Adding up all the named persons, the great armies, the crowds and mobs and those referred to only under general terms such as "the populace", it was shown that the number of people indirectly mentioned in the Bible was actually greater than previously existing estimates of the world population at that time.

Counter-arguments were soon advanced (in a debate which was as acrimonious as its subject was holy). Where in the Bible (one scholar asked) do we find the people of Tahiti, or Brazil? Several ambiguous verses were duly furnished. And can we be sure that the large number of souls who inhabit the pages of that book are not in fact a much smaller group who are simply mentioned on numerous occasions? The argument rumbled on.

Nevertheless, the Editors were forced to concede that a chronological ordering was fraught with difficulties. Their next scheme was hardly more successful. Noting that their numbering system was in fact inferior to the usual custom of fore-and surname, since all information on parentage was lost, they opted for a method in which the identities of both parents would be encoded in the address of the offspring (and hence, by extension, the entire ancestry of any child would form its name). They did this by proposing a great Tree of the human race, with our two progenitors placed at the top and once more numbered 1 and 2. Cain and Abel were then called 121 and 122; the last digit denoting the order in which they were born, the first two indicating their parentage. Problems of chronology were immediately overcome, but others remained. The addresses soon became inordinately long (more than two thousand digits after only seven generations). And there were still those troublesome gaps to deal with; the unknown people who resisted all attempts to trace them — that great bulk of the human family who had lived and worked and died without ever warranting the slightest mention in any text; who had laboured in vain, and then vanished into dust and total oblivion. Were they even worth numbering?

Tremendous efforts were made; the Editors found it necessary to employ a great many staff (diverting them from other equally important tasks) in order to pursue their goal. It had quickly become apparent that while the numbers of the dead and forgotten may be vast, those of the remembered are mighty also. On average (they discovered) a single book will refer to 58.3 individuals (real or invented – another task for the Editors). Even the most modest library, then, plays host to more people than a large city.

These citizens of history were soon posing all sorts of problems for the researchers who were seeking to label them appropriately according to their lineage. Socrates talks to a slave – who was this slave? In which foreign territory had his father been captured? Alexander the Great mounts his horse – but who has made the saddle? Who holds the reins while the King mounts? Who combs the horse – and who gave birth to all of these people? They all had to be found and numbered.

It was necessary to deal somehow with that great ocean of half-remembered lives, those lacunae in the Tree of Humanity. Several attempts were made to resolve the difficulties; special codes were invented which would indicate unknown parentage. An entirely new system was even proposed, in which the digits indicated not necessarily one's lineage, but the respective probabilities of all possible lineages. This system, beautiful as it was (and it gave rise to an entirely new branch of mathematics) nevertheless proved impossible to implement.

In the course of five years, the Editorial Committee of the Dictionary of Identity gave catalogue numbers (under one or other system) to some twenty million souls. At the end of it, after their various schemes which might represent the interrelatedness of ourselves one to each other had all proved hopelessly unwieldy, they wondered whether it would have been better to leave things to random choice: to label people simply in the order that they came up for inspection. Faced with such a tangle of relationships and cross-relationships, it seemed that the difference between total order and total chaos is one so fine as to be virtually impossible to distinguish.

And this was when the Editorial Committee conceived at last the proper course for their subsequent research. To catalogue all humanity, place each person in his or her place, was a task made impossible (despite its enormity) only by the scarcity of data. They therefore decided to approach the problem from the other direction.

To begin with, they made the crucial observation that the number of possible human beings is finite. This notion was of course fiercely opposed by certain scholars, who took the evidence of mankind's variety as an obvious counter-argument, but the proof of the thesis was not difficult. A human being is bounded in extent, composed of a finite number of basic units, or "cells" (it is possible that the cells themselves are determined by the permutations of some more fundamental principle, whose variety is even more strictly limited). Given that we are finite, then there can only be a certain maximum number of possible arrangements of the cells by which we are constructed. This, then, was the great plan which the Editorial Committee would now pursue. They would map the totality of these combinations. Their Dictionary would be a listing of all possible human beings, classified according to a systematic enumeration of the permutations of their cells, and with an indication of whether each possible arrangement had yet been realised in human form.

The scale of the undertaking was growing at a rate which could barely be grasped. And yet the perfection and completeness of the proposed task was something which the Editorial Committee found hard to resist. They envisaged fame and immortality; they imagined their own entries, their own classification, in which certain happy combinations of cells might give rise to genius and wisdom. They saw themselves mirrored in their own work; their own identities revealed in far greater depth than they could ever have perceived. And when they were questioned on the feasibility of their undertaking, or its usefulness to mankind, they were not short of justification. The Dictionary of Identity would produce undreamt-of advances in the fields of medicine, philosophy and history. Certain cell combinations (that is to say, certain types of combinatorial address) would be shown to lead to disease or moral corruption, others to saintliness. It would be found that the nobility and heroism of a Charlemagne was encoded not only in his blood, but in the arrangement of every fibre, every muscle and sinew, every nerve and tendon of his body; likewise the treachery of Brutus, the simple piety of St Francis. And these arrangements of cells, these combinatoria would somehow be determined by some more fundamental method of organisation which the Editorial Committee would – they hoped – be able to unravel.

How would they begin this classification of souls? How would they identify a possible soul with an actual one? These were all problems inviting further research, further time, further funds. It would be done, eventually. And what would they arrive at? A complete catalogue of the human race – all those who had lived, who were now alive, or who might ever be born. Could there be any greater object of study than the totality of mankind?

But a problem presented itself almost immediately; only a few days, in fact, after the meeting of the Editorial Committee which made the decision to embark upon the project. A member of the Committee went outside to take the air; he walked along the street where couples strolled and traders briskly went about their business. The boy sweeping the street, the old woman bent like a rusty pocketknife, the young dandy with his cane; these were all combinatoria, mere possibilities in a sea of even greater possibilities. This Committee member went as far as the park, walked beneath the wrought iron arch of its gate. The trees, the birds, these too were arrangements of cells; perhaps some time in the future they would also come to be mapped and catalogued. Even the clouds overhead – might they somehow be reducible to a finite number of steps, to some simple rule or principle which would allow their nebulous form to be subjected to classification?

He sat down on a bench. His own life he now saw as a finite chain of events, outcomes, chances taken or lost. Had all this been determined at the moment of his birth – or at his conception, even? That he would, perhaps, suffer a heart attack on some particular day in the future (the not-too-distant future, perhaps); or that his teeth would rot, his hair turn grey and fall out – it was all no more than the content of that awful message which he now carried, latent and menacing, in his own body. And was his life then no more than the playing out of a scheme, a single possibility, which was ultimately determined by the finite arrangement of certain cells, or certain cells within those cells; a permutation which was itself laid down by the cells of his parents, or else simply by chance? Was the whole world no better than the throw of a die?

He felt a strange heaviness. Everything around him, if it really was so ruthlessly explicable, if it really was reducible to chance, or to nothing, seemed suddenly worthless. And then at last, as his speculations carried him into ever deeper realms of despair, he looked up. Sitting now on the bench opposite, he saw two young children with their governess; two girls, of about five or six. They were twins, completely identical, inseparable to the closest inspection. Each one dressed in the same blue frills, the same hat; each with identically blond hair (even the curls seemed to match), and from their two faces, identical copies looked out of blue eyes, innocent and infinitely appealing.

And that Committee member could see at once the limitations of what had been proposed. You can construct the same human being twice, and get two entirely different people. These girls would grow up, one might be proud and haughty, the other shy; one might die of love, the other go into a nunnery. Who could say? The construction of their bodies was only the first stage; they would now be further constructed by the events around them, by the accidents of fate which would push them this way or that. By the smile of the governess, as she leaned over them and offered each a sweet pastry from the box on her lap. Why did she offer first to the child who sat furthest from her? Had she already formed a favourite, and if so, how? (How can one make a preference between two supposedly identical beings?) And if she had chosen a favourite, how would their differing treatment now amplify the differences between the two girls – make one cheerful, the other jealous?

He went back to the Committee room, and told them what he had seen. Could one ever identify a genius or a criminal, a poet or a soldier by nothing more than the arrangement of certain biological data? A fierce argument ensued – the individual might be predisposed by nature towards certain characteristics; a born criminal would emerge as such even in the healthiest family, and so on. But it was clear that the Dictionary of Identity would have to be expanded still further. The Index of Bodily Composition was only its first branch. One would also need to consider the Anthology of Possible Lives.

And this is what we all now work on. For the last twelve years our efforts have been directed towards the grand dream of classifying the full range of human possibility, of which our own existence is the merest fraction. I am still sometimes visited by that heaviness which overwhelmed me as I sat in the park long ago; it is a heaviness brought on not by the limitations in principle of human life (for I see now that although finite, the possibilities are of vast extent), but rather it is the restrictions under which I myself carry on through life which give me cause for sorrow. Everything is possible, or almost everything; and yet my life has proceeded within the most narrowly determined confines. I could have been an adventurer or a pirate; and yet I am an archivist and researcher – a path which was already clear to me when I was little more than a child. Is this the legacy of my bodily constituents after all?

That, however, is a topic which must be considered elsewhere, by other writers; those, for instance, who now study the brain and all its possible forms and modes of operation. My current observations are ended, and I shall return to my work.

Goldmann said, "What did the stranger's manuscript contain?"

"I can't quite remember now; all I know is that it was something about a Dictionary. And the poor fellow who showed me it seemed to take very seriously the idea that he may have come from an imaginary city."

"It sounds as though he may have lost his reason as well as his memory."

"Perhaps. Although I was of course aware that his philosophical position was entirely respectable, if a little absurd. I said to him, 'In your imaginary city do they slurp real soup as loudly as you have just done?'"

The stranger frowned. "Forgive me sir, if all that I say appears to make no sense. All I know is that I woke up in a ditch some days ago, that I carry certain obscure documents, and that I have no idea where they come from or for whom they are intended. My speculations are further fuelled, though not resolved, by the existence among my papers of a letter, written in a different hand from my own, which bears no indication either of its sender nor the intended recipient."

Sir,
For many years you have ignored or dismissed me, and so I do not expect to be treated any differently on this occasion. The universe, as I have indicated repeatedly, extends far beyond the narrow boundaries which your so-called Encyclopaedia would set for it. You have tried to devote your life to Reason, neglecting those senses and passions which, if you had allowed yourself to yield to them, might have brought you greater wisdom and

happiness. You have given up many years of your life, so it is said, to a woman who merely used you. Now, in your old age, only Memory is left to you, and that faculty can hardly provide much comfort, since you know (from the evidence I have sent you) that your theories are fallacious, your physics quite unfounded. The universe cannot be explained by all your theorems and principles, your dry mechanics. Rather it is governed by chance and necessity, by the laws of possibility.

Your arid view of the world is so lacking in Imagination, that third faculty which in your scheme was little else than a repository for arts which you found no more than merely entertaining. Yet Imagination is in reality the most important branch of all, since it is the one by which we truly construct the universe which we choose to inhabit.

You and your colleagues have seen fit to reject and ridicule my work; however I have found others who are more sympathetic, and I have compiled the writings of a great many scholars, both ancient and contemporary, whose opinions are of a sort which you would dismiss, but which nevertheless extend human comprehension far beyond anything you can conceive. Your work is finite by its very nature, and though it may win respect, it will be forgotten. The task which I have set myself, however, is limitless in scope, it will be continued by others after my death, and has a value which can never diminish. You and your colleagues have sought to reduce everything to a few meaningless axioms; we, on the other hand, have set out to build an entire universe.

Pfitz asked the stranger, "What does the letter mean?"

"I don't know. I suppose that I may be the emissary of its author, but other interpretations could be equally valid."

"And what do you intend to do now that you've filled your flask with water and your stomach with soup?"

"I thank you for your hospitality. I shall continue walking, in the hope that I shall arrive at a place where the nature of my mission may at last become apparent to me."

Before leaving, he showed Pfitz more of his papers. There were accounts of strange languages and customs, crafts and technology, and descriptions of that imaginary city which the traveller believed himself to have come from, among which Pfitz read the following:

The astronomical clock is the most prominent feature of the tower, being the natural point of attraction for anyone who should care to view the square, and the buildings which both occupy and define it. The tower itself, and the town hall which it adjoins, are imposing but not exceptional, resembling many other edifices of similar purpose. The clock, however, is a wonder quite unique in the subtlety of its conception, and the perfection of its manufacture.

The automata perched on the tower, which strike bells, raise swords or otherwise spring to life at appropriate intervals, are little more than ingenious toys to delight the common crowd. The sculpted skeleton who sways his scythe on the hour may be quite potent as a *memento mori*, but is really just a decoration, an amusing diversion from the mysteries of the clock face (or rather, of its many interconnected faces). Likewise the lifeless soldiers whose halberds clash noiselessly (without any warlike anger) every hour, just after the skeleton's performance; these too do little more than provide low entertainment for those who cannot understand the ways and mechanism of the clock. If there is any moral to be drawn from their endlessly repeated repertoire of meaningless gestures, it is that those who watch are themselves part of some greater cycle, just as invisible to them as the turning of the hours is to those mute wooden figures.

From the clock, it is possible to learn far more than the current time of day. The date is also there, indicated by a pointer which crawls around the outer edge of the clockface at a rate of one revolution per year. Similarly the season is indicated, by a slowly changing picture set within the dial, and also the hours of sunrise and sunset. Other data abound, and this wealth of information is made possible by the fact that the clock does not bear two hands pivoted at the centre, as is usual in such machines. Rather, the dial of the clock contains (that is, it encompasses) a further set of non-concentric moving discs which overlap and are set one upon the other in a most intricate and cunning way. It is by studying the points where the edges of these various discs meet that one can obtain the desired information.

The hour is marked by the largest of the moving discs; it proceeds around the main dial, with its edge progressively touching the fixed numbers set in Roman script about the clockface. This hour-disc itself turns during its course, and a series of levers connected to it can then plot the positions of the sun and moon.

Quite how many discs there are upon the clock I cannot say exactly; the form in which they overlap and connect is very complicated, and one can never see all of them at a given moment (as far as I know). It is also difficult to keep track of which disc is which, in order to be able to count them. Indeed, I have often wondered whether the creator (or creators) of the clock were not somehow able to design the machine in such a way that the discs became interchangeable, performing more than one function at different times. This might account for the way in which so much complexity can be achieved in a relatively compact space.

Apart from the positions of the sun and moon (including the phases of the latter), one can also follow those of the planets (which move through beautifully represented images of the zodiacal constellations) and of the stars themselves. When the existence of a new planet was recently postulated by one of our astronomers, it was noticed that such a body does indeed exist already on the clock, in the predicted orbit. From this, one can conclude that the clock is built to a standard of rigour and perfection matched only by nature itself (if not actually exceeding it). Rather than continue to study the heavens, we might propose instead to devote all our attentions to a full elucidation of the clock and its workings, for this would seem to imply an equal if not superior wealth of discovery.

Like any other timepiece, the astronomical clock is based on the idea of repeating cycles, and the overlapping of these cycles. The hours, days, years; these are all ultimately circular in form, by virtue of their repetition. What makes our clock so extraordinary is that it can also measure things which exhibit no repetition or regularity; which would otherwise, in fact, seem irrational and without meaning (since our common notions of rationality and meaning are based on the ideas of repetition and repeatability). One small disc (discovered only recently) marks out a seemingly random course across the clock face. This particular dial, no bigger than a coin, is fixed on a strut whose ultimate pivot lies hidden somewhere beneath the tangle of discs and levers which obscure the centre of the great clockface. The little coin-disc (barely visible from the square below) must, we assume, owe its motion to some fundamental regularity, and yet its path is wayward, hesitant and irregular. The purpose of this particular component is still unknown, but it has been suggested that it (and others which are now being located) might somehow indicate aspects of our own past and future. Already it is well known that the clock displays in order every Pope beginning with Peter, and also every major conflict, plague and famine. That other historical details are there if only we can find them seems to be beyond doubt, but the prospect that the future likewise is indicated on the clockface is both disturbing and profound. One consequence of this may be that the whole of human history is itself some kind of great cycle, which can be marked as easily as the passing of a single hour, or a single day.

Naturally, there have been many attempts to reduce the infinite subtlety of the astronomical clock to a simple description of its mechanism. This task has, however, so far proved impossible. Those who have been allowed to scale the outer wall of the tower in order to examine the clockface in close detail have found this method of investigation to be utterly futile. Viewed from close quarters (these brave people aver) the devices which adorn the face are so numerous and intricate that they can no longer be seen to have any meaning at all. It is only from ground level, when one may appreciate the apparatus in its entirety, that a coherent pattern can be discerned. Of those who have scaled the walls to look closer, only one has found himself able to construct any kind of theory which is not wholly ludicrous, and this merely concerns the workings of a single insignificant component (a rather minor disc which shows the time of day in Jerusalem).

An inspection of the clock's interior is equally fruitless. The tower was in fact sealed up very thoroughly some time after the manufacture of the machine, but curiosity proved too much for one administration during our history, and the stones which had been put in place in order to block the stairs were removed. A further series of barriers were discovered, which took some two years to overcome. Many were simply decoys, hiding the entrance to passages which in the end led nowhere, so that it seemed at one stage as if the mechanism of the clock would never be located. However, a system of chambers was eventually found and broken into, in which was discovered the most chaotic assemblage of gears and chains. Despite many months of careful study, no sense could be made of their intricacies. Indeed, how does one ever make sense of a piece of machinery, except by watching the outcome of its operation? Thus the attempt to understand the clock by investigating its workings was doomed from the very start, since in order to comprehend the motion of those inscrutable gears, one must first elucidate fully the purpose of the wandering discs which inhabit the clockface – the very object of the enquiry. It was suggested by some that an appropriate course of action would be selectively to disable certain specified parts of the machinery, and then see what effect this would have on the movement of the clockface. This plan, however, was held to be far too dangerous to attempt, since the task of repairing a machine which no-one fully understands would probably be an impossible one, while the destruction of the clock would be a crime of incalculable magnitude.

No pendulum was discovered inside the tower, nor any other source of motion by which the clock might be regulated or driven. It has been postulated that the influence of the wind or sun may maintain the action of the clock (though how this occurs, no-one has been able to explain); as for some source of time from which it might draw steady progress, the theories of those who have studied the matter are numerous and varied. The passing of the sun, in addition to giving power to the mechanism, may also provide the clock with its sense of time (the device having been calibrated to mark by one day the period after which the sun returns). More radical, however, is the idea that the clock may be wholly independent of the need for pendula, or the sun, or any other external form of periodicity. The clock may (it is conjectured) perceive and measure time in a manner which is absolute and irreducible; analogous to the intuitive understanding of time which is experienced by the human mind, yet without the weakness of inaccuracy by which we are constantly beset. The clock would then have to be regarded as far more than a mere measuring device, but rather as a sort of mind, having its own intelligence and understanding of the world which it inhabits. I regard such speculations as fanciful and insupportable; nevertheless, the problem remains of explaining just how it is that this fantastic machine is able to calculate every form of celestial motion without so much as a pendulum to regulate it.

The identity of the clock's original author is unknown, though many suggestions have been put forward, none of which has been able to withstand closer examination. No comparable work exists anywhere else in the world, and it is impossible to trace some lineage of craftsmanship of which the clock would be the pinnacle. It cannot be any older than the tower which it occupies, and this tower cannot have stood for more than two or three centuries. At least, such a date is based upon what is known about the adjoining town hall. On the other hand, it may be the case that the tower in fact predates the hall, rather than vice versa (as is commonly supposed, more by convention than on the basis of any firm evidence).

Sculptors have detected in the poses of the automata the influence of Slavic art, but this cannot be taken to imply anything about the clock itself, since it would have been quite usual for the machinery and decoration to have been constructed independently. As for the clock face, with its overlapping discs and lesser dials, here a number of distinct stylistic trends have been identified. For example, the Roman numerals which surround the entire face are of a different pattern from those adorning the third lunar disc (the number four being represented by IV or IIII). Similarly, the figures of Adam and Eve on the mysterious Disc of the Furies (as it is known to scholars) are done in a manner wholly unlike that of the soldiers on the underlying Disc of Perihelia. This has led several students to the conclusion that the clock was in fact constructed over a considerable period of time (a century or more, according to some). Taking such an idea to its limit, one may conjecture that the clock is not the invention of a single mind, but has instead emerged as the product of countless men's labours; the result being far greater than anything which even the highest genius could achieve through solitary effort. Each successive craftsman may have understood the way in which his own addition to that growing nest of discs might operate and interconnect with the other machinery, and yet be unable to calculate the full effect of his contribution. Thus it would be, that the functions of the clock may be more than was intended; data may lie hidden in its workings which have been put there by no-one.

For all its great age, and the many years during which the clock has looked down on the square and the grand buildings which surround it, our understanding of the clock is still in its infancy. Every evening I go to look at it, standing amongst the crowd which habitually gathers to be entertained by the toy figures and ringing bells, and as I gaze up at the impenetrable richness of the clockface I find myself contemplating once more the subtle works of that first Author, made manifest before me in a manner which is symbolic and yet no less real. And I imagine the day, far in the future, when the last secrets of the clock will finally have yielded themselves to human understanding; when every motion, and every cycle within another cycle, will be described and explained in terms of some underlying geometry about which we know as yet only the barest details. That distant age will be a time of peace and wisdom, when all the ignorance by which men suffer will at last have been eradicated. And perhaps when that era comes (a hundred years from now, or a thousand, or a hundred thousand) then our descendants might fathom that still greater mystery, beyond the question of how it is that the clock operates and what it tells us: namely the question of exactly what it is that the clock measures; what time consists of, and where it goes once it has passed.

Meanwhile, we are left to ponder and speculate upon the infinite intricacy of those wandering discs; slowly moving, and overlapping in ways whose complexity suggests constantly the promise of some underlying unity, some hidden secret by which everything may be elucidated. And we are left to try and guess what cycle it might be (or nest of cycles) which defines the irregular course of our own lives; on what insignificant disc, supported by what unknown levers, we are propelled through time in a space which has in fact the form of some giant dial, some immeasurable clockface, perfectly circular and rationally divided, and representing a machine which is complete, indivisible, and yet quite beyond hope of comprehension.

IV

"It's a pity that I can't remember any of the things the stranger showed me," Pfitz told Goldmann. "Afterwards he put all of his documents back into his satchel, and then left."

"The poor fellow," said Goldmann. "I wonder what became of him."

"Either he died, or else he will die, or else he never existed."

"Oh Pfitz, you really are depressing. Didn't you feel any sympathy for him?"

"To tell the truth I almost envied him. I often think how good it would be to lose my own memory, or at least some of it; there's so much up there that just lies around without ever getting used, it would be handy to be able to make a bit more space."

Goldmann cried, "You treat so casually the suffering of others!" After this outburst, he could find no further words, nor did Pfitz attempt to defend or excuse himself. For a long time, they sat in silence, and Goldmann's anxiety crept back until he began to find it increasingly difficult to hold at bay the sense of despair which their unpleasant situation invited. When would they be released? And whatever would his wife say? The silence only made his anxiety greater. At last he felt forced to speak.

"Tell me another story Pfitz. Anything."

"Will you pay?"

"Later. I've no money left."

"All right then." Pfitz thought for a moment. "Two people meet by chance, at the bottom of a garden. That's how the story begins; she lives in a chateau, and every day her nanny takes her to school. They walk together down the big path, and on through the gardens. He sees her going past each day, wonders who she is, where she's going and so on."

"Is she pretty?"

"Does it matter?"

"No, I suppose not," said Goldmann. "Though you usually expect them to be pretty in stories like that."

"Stories like what? I've hardly started. And anyway, ugly people fall in love too, you know."

"Of course, I'm sorry. I didn't mean to offend you."

"Why ever should I be offended? I was thinking of the Countess Podolski."

"Let's get back to the story, Pfitz. I don't care what she looked like, all I know is that she used to go down through the garden every day, when her nanny took her from the chateau. Can you tell me how old she was?"

"I don't know. Old enough to fall in love, I suppose."

"And how old is that?"

"You tell me. I've been falling in love since I was too young to remember."

"But don't we get some kind of hint? A clue in the story?"

"Well, we know she has a nanny who takes her to school. That limits things. But the nanny could be more like a kind of chaperone or companion. The story is a translation, of course, so maybe the word which gets translated as nanny is really more specific in the original. In fact, the school itself might have crept in through mistranslation too – or even the entire tale, come to that. But does it really matter how old she is, or whether she's pretty or ugly? Can't you just accept a story at face value?"

"I like to see things in my head Pfitz, and if the story is too vague then I won't be able to see anything at all. Or else the things I do see will begin to contradict each other; for example there's a pretty five year old girl getting taken through a garden when suddenly she's fifteen and has a face like a horse's arse."

"There's no need to be rude about her."

"I'm sorry. But what about the rest of the story? They meet in a garden – then what?"

"Do you have to keep interrupting and jumping the gun, sir? How can you expect me to develop my theme if you won't allow me to start properly?"

"I know. Forgive me for being so impatient Pfitz, but all this waiting, while nothing happens. It makes me – I don't know what."

"Nervous, perhaps?"

"No. Certainly not. We're sure to be released soon. But sitting here like this for so long, I feel . . . fidgety I suppose."

"I can't see you fidgeting," said Pfitz.

"But my insides are fidgety – because they're impatient to hear about this damned girl and her nanny!"

"When your insides are fidgety then I call that being nervous."

"Stop being so irritating and just tell me the bloody story. All I know is that a girl and a boy meet in a garden and they fall in love."

"I never said that."

"But that's what happens, isn't it?"

"Well sir, if you know everything before I even tell it then I might as well save my breath, don't you think?"

"They obviously do fall in love, though."

"I don't see what's obvious about it at all. Just because they meet at the bottom of a garden you assume they fall in love.

A huge assumption, if you ask me. Do you fall in love with everyone you meet at the bottom of a garden?"

"If I were a character in a story then I probably would, otherwise there'd be no point in my being there. But very well, they meet in a garden, and it's the kind of story where you think they're going to fall in love, but then they don't after all."

"I never said that."

"Then what kind of a story is it?"

"What kind? It's the kind of story that creeps up on you, almost without you realising it, about two people who meet by chance. You don't know anything about them – what they look like, how they dress, or even what age they live in."

"Fine! Keep going!"

"Thank you, I will. They meet – by chance – quite near the beginning of the story. Or perhaps even before the beginning, because it's sometimes a bit difficult to say exactly when two people first meet. Maybe they've been together already for some time without noticing each other. And sometimes it's also difficult to know where the beginning of a story really is, or the ending, because what you hear seems to come from somewhere in the middle."

"Get on with it, Pfitz. Just hurry up and get to the end."

"I already have."

"What?"

"I didn't mention that it's the kind of story that just stops suddenly."

"Pfitz, you're an imbecile and a rogue and . . . and . . ." but Goldmann could not finish. Instead he burst into tears, so that Pfitz had to put a comforting arm round him.

"I'm sorry sir. But what can you expect when you try to buy a story from me on credit?"

The stress of captivity was clearly affecting Goldmann deeply, and Pfitz took pity on him. "Don't worry, sir, we'll be released soon. Remember I've been through all of this before, when they arrested me during the Corn Tax riot."

"But what about the awful story of the doll, and the man who was hanged?"

"Oh, I made it all up. Actually when I turned round to the man beside me, he said his name was Schlick, not Schmidt." Pfitz described how they were sitting there in the cell; he and Schlick on the floor while others were on the stone benches or pacing nervously. "Tell me," Pfitz had said to him, "how is it that you have come to find yourself here?" And then Schlick had begun to tell his story.

"I was born in a village not far from here. My father was a schoolmaster, a good and kindly man, and I was the seventh of eleven children, only five of whom survived to adulthood. My mother did her best to keep us all adequately clothed and fed, though as you can well imagine it wasn't an easy task. Even so, they raised us decently, and put us firmly on the path of righteous living. No alcohol was ever allowed in the house, and every evening my father would read to us from the family Bible. On Sundays we would go together to the church, all of us children marching in line behind our father, and from the words of the Pastor and the simple melodies of the hymns I drew profound lessons which have remained with me all my life.

"When I was twelve I became an apprentice teacher at the school, and by the age of sixteen was supervising lessons on my own. I was destined to follow my father's worthy example. And then I met Martha. Her father regularly visited our village to sell vegetables, and would bring his daughter to help him count the money he took. That was how I first saw her — sitting beside her father on their wagon. I fell in love with her immediately.

"I soon discovered the pattern of their visits. On the first Tuesday of every month they would set up stall in the village square, remaining there throughout the afternoon. Around two o'clock was the best time to watch Martha; the square would be busy, and I need not fear being noticed while I carried out my observation from a nearby corner.

"At this stage I still did not even know her name, but her face filled my thoughts constantly. Then one night I dreamt that I was alone in a strange house. It was dark, except for the light of the moon which cast long shadows across the walls and features of the unknown place. I got up, and began to move about between the rooms, exploring the eerie building in which I found myself. It was a huge house, with many more corridors and doors than I could ever hope to investigate. Thinking back, I realise that what this house contained were all of my possible lives. Many of the doors were locked; I struggled with the handles, trying in vain to pull them open. Behind some of them, I could hear distant voices or laughter, or music. Behind others, the sound of children playing or crying. At last, I found one that I could open.

"Inside, I saw Martha sitting in a rocking chair, gently swaying back and forth. She looked up, and said she had an important message for me. Then she began to tell me how her father, who brought her every month on his wagon, had subjected her on many occasions to a kind of cruelty whose name I dare not even speak. She begged me to help her, but when I tried to reply I found that from my open mouth no sound could emerge except a dry rasping. Then she took my hand and led me through another door at the back of the room, where I found a blood-soaked bed, upon which her father lay dead with a knife in his breast.

"Appalled by the horror of this sight I ran back out into the corridor and closed the door behind me, holding fast against Martha's attempts to reopen it from where she remained inside. At last her struggling ceased.

"I went along the corridor past several more locked doors, until I found another which I could open. In this room I saw Martha once more, sitting at a table with her father over a meal of boiled turnips. They both looked round at me, and laughed. I awoke."

"Had he been eating cheese before he went to bed?" asked Goldmann. "I find it always gives me nightmares such as he described. A glass of hot milk helps settle the stomach."

Pfitz continued to describe the story he had heard. Schlick

was speaking softly to him, and all the others in the cell were now listening patiently.

"The dream left a great impression on me. I waited for the next time Martha would come to our village, and when the day arrived I went to the square, determined to speak with her. She was there with her father as usual, selling vegetables from the wagon. I watched from a distance the movement of her body as she passed goods down to customers, took their money, gave it to her father. I watched the curve of her back, and the stretching of the white blouse she wore. I watched, and I delighted in the happy scenes which my mind invented, until I recalled once again my ghastly dream. Her father, meanwhile, was busy with other customers. I saw my chance.

"I approached the wagon. He was talking to someone on the other side; she had just given some change to an old man. Before she could do anything else, I took her hand. She looked at me, startled and speechless. Her eyes were so dark they seemed like black pools, infinitely trusting. 'I know everything,' I said, and squeezed her hand before making my escape, leaving her to continue with her work.

"That night, I dreamt once more that I was in the strange house, whose rooms and passages extended in every direction. I went in search of Martha, knowing somehow which way to go, which turning to take, which door to open. I found myself inside a mirrored chamber. The floor, ceiling, the four walls; each was a mirror, so that I now saw myself reflected infinitely far, image within image, until my repeated reflection was reduced to the tiniest dot. I went close to one of the walls − one of the mirrors − and pressed my face against its cold glass, so that my breath clouded it. With my sleeve I wiped away the mist on the pane, then looked again into the reflections. Between the layers of images, I briefly saw the figure of Martha, trapped and beyond my grasp. I went out, back through the corridors, down the stairs; I ran in search of an exit. I found myself, panting for breath, on the steps of the building. I was in the street.

"It was a dark corner of some great city, and quite deserted. I began to make my way along its damp alleyways. I heard a noise – a movement somewhere. Only a cat, perhaps. Then I came round a corner, and an arm grabbed me from behind. A knife was being held close to my throat. My assailant gripped me so tightly that any movement was impossible.

" 'What do you want?' I gasped. He told me that he had come to kill me. 'But why?'

" 'Because you know. She told me that you had found out about the two of us. And I won't let any man stop us now.'

"I broke free and turned to look at the assassin. It was not Martha's father, but a younger man. I recognised him as someone from my village.

" 'You can't kill me,' I said. 'The mirrors won't let you.' "

Goldmann asked, "What did that mean?"

Pfitz didn't know, but went on describing the story he had heard.

"When I awoke," Schlick had continued, "I realised that I would have to wait another month before I saw Martha again. But there was also something else which needed to be explained, namely the appearance in my dream of Karl, the lad from the village who tried to kill me. I had never trusted the fellow. He was a rough, uncouth type, with a scar down his cheek from some fight. Whatever money he made from labouring and digging went on beer and cards. He was not much older than me – eighteen or nineteen – but liked to think he was something big in the town. And even grown men often seemed afraid of him.

"I found it hard to believe that Martha could have anything to do with a ruffian like that; though I knew the way he could charm girls who should have known better, and I couldn't have been the only one to have noticed how pretty Martha was. The thought of the two of them together made me insane with jealousy.

"Every day, while I taught lessons at my father's school, I

was thinking of ways to thwart Karl. He was bigger than me, stronger, more handsome. I had only my wits, and my good intentions to assist me. Meanwhile I waited for Martha's next visit to our village.

"When the day came, I went to the square, and saw Martha at her usual place. She recognised me immediately, and became agitated at the sight of me. I went over to the wagon, and climbed onto it next to Martha's father. 'If you so much as touch this girl,' I said to him, 'I'll strike you dead.' He was utterly dumbfounded by this, and stared in silence as I jumped back onto the ground. Karl was slouching against a nearby wall. 'And the same goes for you,' I said, walking away.

"I learned later what happened next. Martha's father wanted to know why I had spoken to Karl – what did he have to do with all of this? He called the boy over and they soon got into an argument, with the father accusing Karl of making advances to Martha (all of which she denied). At some point Karl brought out a knife, only as a threat, or to protect himself, but he ended up stabbing Martha's father. Then he ran off, leaving his victim bleeding to death, before the stunned onlookers could even think to stop him.

"Everyone kept asking me afterwards why I had gone up to him like that and said the things I had, and I explained that it was to protect Martha (it was only now that I learned her name from them, and that she was an only child, and that it all happened soon before her sixteenth birthday, when she was due to be married to a man called Lülling). I told them of the cruelty I suspected her to have been subjected to, though now that I said it I felt much less convinced. And they told me that he would never have treated his daugter badly since she was all he had left after his wife died, and now Martha was an orphan. I realised that I might have made a terrible mistake.

"Months passed. Karl had disappeared, and the incident was gradually being forgotten about. Everyone bought their vegetables elsewhere, now that the wagon no longer made its monthly visits. But the other villagers continued to treat me with suspicion. I was a virtual outcast.

"I was walking by the river one evening. It was twilight, and the narrow path between the trees was becoming harder to follow. Suddenly I was grabbed from behind, and a knife was being held close to my throat. I knew it must be Karl. I thought of the mirrors in my dream, and the figure I had seen lost inside them. I imagined that I too might now be lost."

"And he realised," said Pfitz, "that his own life had been no more than a fleeting vision, a figure glimpsed in the ill-defined region between successive images in an endlessly descending multiplicity of reflections, identical yet diminishing, one within the next."

They heard a jingling of keys. Pfitz and Goldmann both stood up. "We're free!" said Goldmann.

"Thank goodness," Pfitz added. "Any longer and I'd have wet myself. Why couldn't they have given us a bucket to use?"

The guard called out Goldmann's name.

"What about my companion?"

"Only you, Goldmann."

He was led back upstairs to see the Officer.

"Herr Goldmann, I understand that you are a respected citizen of Rreinnstadt, and any misdemeanour in which you may have been involved was quite out of character. I am prepared to release you."

"And Pfitz?"

"The beggar? We know nothing about him. I expect we shall have to hang him."

Goldmann cried out. "Have pity on him, sir. He's done nothing wrong!"

"It isn't as simple as that," the Officer said. "To arrest one man wrongfully is unfortunate; two might seem like negligence. I'm sure he must have done something wrong."

"Please, I can stand bail for him. How much do you want?"

The Officer thought carefully. "Bring me a thousand crowns and I'll see what I can do."

Goldmann was led outside to the main gate, where he blinked in the sunshine. A thousand crowns! It was a great deal of money, but there was no choice. He went as quickly as he could back to his house. Minne was startled when she saw his dishevelled appearance.

"Is Frau Goldmann at home?" he asked.

Minne explained that she was receiving guests upstairs. As Goldmann passed the salon, he could hear the banal trilling of his wife's laughter. He went straight to his desk and brought out two rolls of coins, stuffing them hastily down the legs of his trousers, so that Minne raised her eyebrows in surprise at the strange sight of him passing her once more on the stairs. Then he took a carriage to the Fremmelhof.

"Here's the money," he said, laying the coins down before the Officer. One of the guards took him back downstairs to find the prisoner. They arrived at the door to the cell – and saw that it was empty.

"Where has he been taken?" pleaded Goldmann. "Did they hang the poor man after all?"

No one could tell him. They let him look inside the cell, to make sure he really wasn't there. There was no way in which Pfitz could have escaped. All that remained of him was a puddle on the floor. When Goldmann went back out into the street he was filled with sadness. They hadn't even given back his money! They said they'd keep it to make sure he behaved himself.

Goldmann never saw Pfitz again. Word got around of his strange story, so that he had to come up with all sorts of excuses to appease his wife. There were some who said he was mad or had imagined the whole thing, while others claimed Pfitz was a ghost, or a spirit which had been invoked by malicious and unconstrained story telling. It was many years before Goldmann was able to locate once more, in the great Library of Rreinnstadt, the biography of Count Zelneck. He learned from this that the story of Pfitz was apocryphal; that Zelneck almost certainly had no such servant. Whoever Goldmann's companion had been, it surely could not have been Pfitz. This came as some consolation to

Goldmann, who — it should be added — never again saw the dark interior of the Fremmelhof, or went anywhere without telling his wife first. That at least is how the story is told in Müller's *Tales from Rreinnstadt*. I personally cannot vouch for any of it, and must now bring my account to a close, so that those readers wishing further diversion must, I fear, seek it elsewhere.